THE HAUNTING OF EAGLE CREEK MIDDLE SCHOOL

Samantha Wolf Mysteries
#5

TARA ELLIS

ISBN-13: 978-1533325914

ISBN-10: 153332591X

The Haunting of Eagle Creek Middle School

This book is dedicated to YOU, the readers. I feel that one of my largest milestones as an author is to have fans of this series. I cherish your feedback, and I've listened to what you enjoyed the most. Because of that, John and Hunter have bigger roles than originally planned. Cassy has returned, and the pace is very similar to The Mystery of Hollow Inn. Keep the comments coming!

Samantha Wolf Mysteries

1. The Mystery of Hollow Inn
2. The Secret of Camp Whispering Pines
3. The Beach House Mystery
4. The Heiress of Covington Ranch
5. The Haunting of Eagle Creek Middle School
6. A Mysterious Christmas on Orcas Island

Find these and Tara's other titles on her author page!

http://www.amazon.com/author/taraellis

CONTENTS

Samantha Wolf Mysteries   iv

CONTENTS   v

1. A HAUNTINGLY GOOD IDEA   1

2. A GHOSTLY STORY   7

3. THE PECULIAR MRS. POTTS   15

4. BENEFACTORS   28

5. A PIRATE COVE   38

6. THE GHOST OF EAGLE CREEK   49

7. FAMILY TIES   63

8. MOUNTING CLUES   77

9. HOW TO CATCH A GHOST   89

10. PHANTOM SECRETS   97

11. EVIDENCE   113

12. ROADBLOCK   124

13. GOOD DEEDS GONE WRONG   132

14. AYE, MATIES!   141

15. A HALLOWEEN TO REMEMBER   156

ABOUT THE AUTHOR   162

1

A HAUNTINGLY GOOD IDEA

Sam sits low in her seat at a small table, pushing at a corner of the handout until it's no longer a sharp edge. It's a colorful piece of paper, with fun fonts and a professional looking layout. Her Physical Ed teacher, Miss Covington, is good with a word processor. It's their first official newsletter, highlighting the new school club missions and goals.

They're gathered at the back of the school cafeteria. Miss Covington has finally started their first meeting after waiting for nearly an hour, and only three other students showed up. Although a big turnout wasn't expected on a Monday afternoon after school, it's still disappointing.

Wiggling a bit impatiently, Samantha Wolf

leans her head on Ally's shoulder, who's seated to her left. She notes the stark contrast between her own dark brown hair and Ally's bright red curls, before exchanging a knowing look. They then both turn towards Cassy Sanchez on Sam's right.

"What?" Speaking slowly and with an exaggerated drawl, Cassy bats her lashes at them. "I told you that this fundraising club would be for a good cause. I didn't say anything about it being fun and games." Crossing her arms, the olive-skinned girl narrows her eyes and presses her lips together, daring her two friends to disagree.

Sam studies Cassy's dark eyes for a moment, still amazed at the change she's witnessed in her friend. She went from being a shy, bullied girl, to someone who now rivals Sam's stubbornness!

While Sam and Ally have been friends for years, they only started hanging out with Cassy a couple of months ago. But it's the sort of friendship that feels timeless. The twelve-year-old girls all attend seventh grade together at Eagle Creek Middle school. Their first year at the new school has already proven to be exciting, with the three of them solving a generations-old mystery.

Not only did it end up saving Miss Covington's family ranch, but uncovered the truth that revealed their teacher and Cassy were half-sisters.

The past few weeks have been a whirlwind of changes for Cassy. She moved in with her newly found older sister, and is still waiting for all of the state paperwork to be filed. Her grandmother was raising her, but due to worsening dementia, isn't able to care for her any longer. Now, Grams is in a wonderful assisted-living facility, and Cassy has never been happier.

Sam breaks into a wide smile, unable to hold up the charade any longer, and Cassy is quick to smile back. While the school club that Miss Covington created might end up being a tad boring, Cassy is right. It's going to be all about raising money for local charities, not having fun. Unless…

"Oh!" Sam exclaims, surprising even herself with the outburst.

"You have something to share?" While the young teacher's voice is somewhat stern, her face is soft, and she stares at Sam with a crooked grin. She's used to her young student's impulsiveness, and appreciates her spirit.

Blushing slightly, Sam gazes back down at the doodling she's made in the margin of the handout. *Charity club...after school...fundraising ideas.* She writes out *haunted house* below it, and then looks back at Miss Covington, whose short blonde hair is a good match for her petite frame. "A haunted house!" she blurts out, getting more excited now. "Our church put one on a couple of years ago, and raised all sorts of money for the youth group. Halloween is in three weeks. *We* could make a haunted house here, at the school!"

Miss Covington taps at her lips with the eraser end of her pencil for a moment, contemplating the suggestion. "We'll have to talk with our benefactor, Mrs. Potts, about it," she finally says. "The afterschool program she funds is really struggling right now, which is why I chose it. Not only is the success of our first project important for that reason, but the school board has made it clear that the club will get shut down if we don't prove it's possible to raise more than we spend."

Sam has continued to doodle, expanding to drawings of pumpkins and ghosts. She pauses, looking up at her teacher and friend. Sam knows that Miss Covington is donating her own money for the start-up funds. Although she has a large amount of cash coming to her as a result of the girls proving her entitlement to a family inheritance, it will be tied up in probate for several more weeks. Her teacher's salary doesn't go that far after the expenses of living on her old family farm, especially now that she's also supporting Cassy.

"Since all of the local stores already have their decorations for sale, I'll bet we could get some of them to donate stuff, if we explain what it's for," Sam presses, getting more excited about the idea. "And we can have the boys help us. I'm sure they'd love to dress up and scare kids!" 'The boys' are Sam and Ally's older brothers, John and Hunter, who are both in high school.

"What if we made special coupons for the kids at the afterschool program?" Cassy suggests. "If they get to go through the haunted house for free, Mrs. Potts might be more likely to say yes. I know that when I used to go there, the most fun we ever had was going on field trips. The kids would love it!"

Miss Covington's smile has been growing,

and she's starting to write the thoughts down as the girls talk.

"My dad's really into Halloween and all the decorating and stuff," adds one of the boys seated at the other table. Sam doesn't know him or the other two girls, but she's seen them around. He scratches briefly at his blond head, and then turns in his seat to face Miss Covington. "I'm pretty sure we have a bunch of extra skeletons. Probably one of those smoke machine things, too."

"Thank you, Brian," Miss Covington replies, making more notes. "How about all of you think of ways that you can contribute to putting on a haunted house," she says, looking at each of them. "It would be a big project, and we don't have a whole lot of time, but I like the idea! I'll speak with the board tomorrow to see if we can use the gym, and then we'll go talk with Mrs. Potts about it."

Sam claps her hands together in excitement, and then jumps up from the table. "Come on!" she urges Ally, after they say goodbye to Cassy. "Let's go find our brothers. This is going to be the best haunted house *ever*!"

2

A GHOSTLY STORY

"Stop trying to scare your sister." Kathy Wolf points her fork at Hunter for emphasis, but the glop of mashed potatoes falling off the end of it causes smiles around the dinner table, instead of fear.

"But it's *true,* Mom," Hunter counters, his grin widening. He has the same dark eyes and hair of his father, but the short stature of his mom. Sam, on the other hand, is nearly as tall as he is already. Ethan Wolf constantly tries to convince his son that all of the Wolf men start to grow in their later teens, but Hunter believes he's destined to be forever smaller than his friends. "Everyone knows that Eagle Creek Middle

7

School is haunted. Right, John?" Nudging his best friend in the ribs, Hunter shovels more of his dad's famous meatloaf into his mouth.

"Umm...sure," John confirms, glancing briefly at a scowling Mrs. Wolf. His cheeks burning, he sets his own fork down, feeling a need to explain himself. At sixteen, he's two years older than Hunter and has a greater sense of accountability than his friend.

"The story goes, that some fifty years ago, there was a horrible accident in the boiler room under the school."

"Is that what they used for heat?" Ally asks, interrupting her brother.

"Yeah," John confirms. "I think they converted the school to a regular furnace some time ago, but the boiler is still there, because it's too expensive to remove it. Anyway," he continues, looking around the table at his captive audience, "the janitor pretty much worked there his whole life. He knew what he was doing, but that night, something went terribly wrong and he died in the mishap. Ever since, on cold nights, you can hear the sounds of his ghost wandering the basement under the school, trying to fix the boiler."

"Oh, please," Sam laughs it off. "That's not even all that impressive, as far as ghost stories go! But…" pausing with her glass of water halfway to her mouth, she slams it back down and spins towards Ally. "We should use that in the haunted house!" she shouts, bouncing in her chair. "Have John dress up in an old janitor suit, or something."

"Uhhmm," Ethan clears his throat loudly, while staring pointedly at his daughter. "Samantha, do you really think that would be in good taste?"

"Yeah, *Samantha*," Hunter adds, not missing a chance to tease his sister. "Why would we want to waste our time running around in a stupid kid's thing, anyway?"

"Because it's for a good cause," Ally argues. "And I agree with your dad," she adds, turning back to Sam. "If someone really did die, I wouldn't want to make light of it. There's a ton of other things we can have them dress up as," she quickly ads, seeing the defeated look on Sam's face. "John would make a good Frankenstein!"

Sticking his arms out in front of him, John does a pretty good impersonation, groaning loudly and causing squeals of laugher from Abigail and Tabitha, Sam's two-year-old twin sisters. Their blonde heads bob in unison, little miniature images of their mother.

Her brief moment of despair gone, Sam laughs along with her sisters at John's antics. The large dining room table barely accommodates them all, but they recently fell into the habit of having Ally and John over for dinner on Monday nights. They live only two houses apart, so it's a normal occurrence for the kids to be at one or the others home. Since John and Ally's parents are often gone working, the Wolfs' cozier house is usually the first choice. Her dad also prides himself for his cooking, and Monday is his night to show off.

Sam's mood darkens again, as she watches her dad joking with Hunter. He'll be leaving for Alaska next month, where he works as a commercial fisherman. The much-needed income is a necessity, especially since her mom quit her job as a teacher to stay home with the twins. Normally, he would have already left, going after halibut. But his role with his employer evolved over this past summer, and now he's been put in charge of the big king crab run that begins November first. After that, he's going to stay on to oversee some of the smaller shrimping operations, until the pacific cod season starts in January. He'll be home for Christmas, but then he won't come back until spring, and Sam always misses him so much when he's gone.

The thought of spring pulls her reflections in a different direction, and Sam feels a small stirring of excitement. Miss. Covington has big plans for her old horse ranch, high on the hill not far from their home. Once she gets her inheritance, Lisa Covington can make some much-needed repairs to the estate. But that's just the beginning. Sam, Ally, and Cassy have already agreed to help clear the miles of trails in the woods, in preparation for a summer riding school that Lisa wants to run.

It's still weird to think of her as Lisa, Sam acknowledges. Her teacher insisted that the girls call her by her actual name when they're not at school. It's easy for Cassy to make the transition, since she's her sister, but it's harder for Sam and

Ally to follow suit. However, the more time they spend together at the ranch, the more natural it becomes. They'll be there a bunch this summer, since Sam gets to help take care of the horses that Lisa is going to be getting.

It's always been Sam's dream to have a horse of her own. They have an old barn back in the corner of their three-acre lot, but not the money needed to take care of a horse. Now, Sam will have a chance to spend a whole summer riding and training!

A light hand on her arm draws Sam from her daydreams, and she turns to find Ally studying her.

"What are you thinking about?" Ally asks, tilting her head slightly. "You look like you're on another planet."

"Horses."

Sam and Ally are close enough that no further explanation is needed, and they simply exchange a knowing smile.

Sam then absently smears a chunk of meatloaf into some ketchup, but still fails to take a bite when she spots the pile of football gear by the backdoor. Although Hunter is a freshman at the high school and on the JV team while his older friend is on varsity, he and John still get to practice together.

"What if," she says loudly, interrupting the current conversation about how to properly barbeque a salmon, "you guys wore your football gear?"

"Huh?" Hunter responds, clearly not following her line of questioning.

"In the haunted house," Sam presses. "Do you think your coach would let you wear it? We could do your makeup to make you look like zombies!"

John runs a hand through his blonde hair, his blue eyes sparkling back at Sam. "That's not a half-bad idea," he states. "It might be kinda fun, Hunter," he adds. "I think the coach would be okay with it. We do worse things to it every game."

"Maybe." Hunter hesitates, thinking about the possibilities. "I guess if I got to scare a bunch of kids it wouldn't be too boring."

"And you'd get all the candy you want!" Ally throws in, knowing the direct way to Hunter's heart.

"Done!" he agrees, and then promptly goes back to cleaning off his plate.

3

THE PECULIAR MRS. POTTS

The elegant, cobblestone driveway is both long and steep, and as a light rain begins to soak into her sweatshirt, Sam wishes that they'd parked closer to the large estate on the top of the hill.

Even hunched over against the chilly fall afternoon, Sam is taller than both of her friends. Cassy is a close second, but Ally is forced to take about two steps for each one of hers, unable to match her long stride. Lisa is pulling away from them all, having decided to jog to the base of the sweeping front steps.

Lisa finally got approval for the haunted house from the school, after three days of debating it with them. There was concern about damage to the newer gym flooring. After promising to put down tarps, they reluctantly agreed, but there's even more pressure now to make it a success.

As soon as she got word from the school board earlier today, Lisa arranged to meet with Mrs. Potts. Once the benefactor says yes to the haunted house idea, they can then move forward with gathering donations and figuring out how they're going to put it all together. Sam feels the first twinges of anxiety over the project. It *is* her idea, after all. If it fails, she'll feel horrible about it.

Lisa is striking the large wooden door with an ornate metal knocker, which looks like an antique and something they could copy for the entrance to the haunted house. Sam grins when she realizes how the layout of the maze on the gym floor, which will be made of cardboard, is already beginning to form in her head. It *will* be good!

The knocking is answered almost immediately, as if the older woman were waiting on the other side of the door. Sam doesn't know what she was expecting, but Mrs. Potts is not at all how she pictured her.

Dressed in pale pink slacks and a white silk blouse, she looks very trim and proper. Her white hair is done up in a large bun, small wisps of it escaping around her face. Although she must be in her late sixties, she has a much younger energy to her, and stands wringing her thin hands while shifting back and forth on the balls of her feet. Glancing briefly over her shoulder down a darkened hallway, she turns back with a small scowl on her otherwise pleasant face when she sees the cluster of girls standing behind their teacher.

"Miss. Covington, I presume?" she asks matter-of-factly. "I wasn't expecting a whole entourage." The comment was obviously directed at the girls, although it wasn't said with malice. It was more like anxiousness.

"Yes! It's so nice to meet you, Mrs. Potts. And please, call me Lisa. This is my sister, Cassy," Lisa continues, guiding Cassy by the shoulders to move up next to her. "And these are my students, Sam and Ally. They're taking key roles in creating the fundraising club. I thought it might be nice to have them present their idea to you. I hope you don't mind. It won't take long."

Realizing that she's at risk of being rude, Mrs. Potts takes a sharp intake of breath and then waves them all inside the large, well-lit foyer. "Oh, of course! It's just that I haven't had company in so long; I've forgotten how to be a gracious host. Please, kick off your wet sneakers and come join me in the sitting room. I have a nice fire going. It's the first time this year I've lit one and I just love the sound of the crackling pine!"

Following behind as Mrs. Potts leads the way, Sam is surprised to find that she's reminded of her Grandma Wolf. She and Grandpa live far enough away in Montana that they only get to visit once every year or two. Grandma Wolf is a tall, gracious, and composed woman. At first, she appears quite strict and rigid. But once you get to know her, she's actually funny and loving. Sam wonders if Mrs. Potts might be the same way, and her original sense of unease is replaced by curiosity.

The sitting room turns out to be exactly what it sounds like: a place to sit. There are two chaise lounges opposite each other, to either side of a large, river-rock fireplace. Facing the fire is an over-stuffed loveseat, big enough for two people to sit comfortably. Based on the blanket and book left on the white cushions, it's obvious that this is where Mrs. Potts prefers to relax.

The furniture completes a square with the fireplace, spaced so that there is plenty of room to walk between them and the large windows that line the walls of the room. The girls stand awkwardly for a moment, hesitant to sit on the immaculate upholstery. Everything in the room is white, from the couches to the walls, and even the carpet … although that's more of a cream tone.

"Please," Mrs. Potts urges, spreading her arms wide to encompass the whole sitting area. "Take a seat. Make yourselves comfortable."

They all move forward at her prompting, with the three young girls crowding together on the far lounge, and Lisa on the other. Mrs. Potts moves her blanket aside before sitting, and sets the paperback on an odd coffee table in the center of the space. Sam notes how the marked and pitted wooden slab seems out of place.

"It's an antique," the older woman explains.

Apparently, she's very observant.

"I like it," Sam says simply, smiling back at their host.

"So," Mrs. Potts continues, turning to Lisa, without offering any further explanation on the table. "You are our new teacher!"

"Yes, I am," Lisa confirms. "I'm originally from the area. The Covington Ranch is my family home."

"Oh, I'm well aware of who you are," she says quickly, waving a hand in the air. "I knew your parents. I'm terribly sorry for all you've been through. I know what it's like to lose someone you love."

Lisa's parents both died in a plane accident when she was sixteen. It ultimately led to the mystery that the girls helped solve just over a month ago, and also the reunion of Cassy with her older sister.

"Thank you, Mrs. Potts," Lisa replies softly. "My condolences to you, too. I remember reading about Mr. Potts' accident. I had moved in with my aunt by then, but it was all over the news. It's not often that we have that big of a storm off our shores!"

Sam struggles with her memory, straining to recall a story she remembers being told on occasion at the dinner table and around the campfire. Lisa didn't shared with them how Mrs. Potts came to be a widow. Before she can decide whether it would be too rude to ask, Cassy is the first to break the silence.

"I hope you don't mind my asking, but what happened?" Lisa shoots Cassy a disapproving look, but Mrs. Potts intervenes before she can scold her.

"It's perfectly all right. I don't mind talking about it. And please," she continues, looking at Lisa, "call me Grace. I might be getting up there in years, but being called Mrs. Potts really makes me feel quite elderly."

Sam smiles at Grace, her first impression of her resembling her grandmother being further solidified. That was totally something she would say. Relaxing a little more, Sam leans back into the plush cushions and listens intently to the story.

"As to my husband's untimely death … I need to preface the story with a couple of things. Our boat company was something we both worked hard for and treasured a great deal. My husband had a difficult start, losing his father at a rather early age. His drive and determination was something few people could match! We built the business into one of the largest in the area, and we both felt obligated to give back to the community. That is how the afterschool program began. It's one of the first charities we founded and the closest to my heart.

"Unfortunately, while my husband was an expert boat-builder and I a marvel at social graces and marketing, neither one of were much of an accountant. I should have hired a professional to handle the books early on, but I was too stubborn to admit I needed help. The summer before the accident, we were in trouble. On the surface, everything ran as usual, but we were paying out more than we were taking in at that point. The market changed. Sure, we still had clients willing to pay for the handcrafted specialty work that Benjamin did, but that wasn't where the money was anymore. Mass market. That's what we needed to tap into, and neither of us knew how.

"Benjamin was working for years on a new

boatbuilding material. It was ingenious, really. Lightweight, inexpensive, but looked as nice as real mahogany. He was convinced it would be our salvation, but a large production company initially turned him down. He needed investors to make it a reality. So that Saturday afternoon, he took his small sailboat, made of this material, out on its maiden journey. He assured me that if he could prove how well it worked, no one could say no.

"It will forever be a question left unanswered. Maybe he was right, but we'll never know."

Her face tightening, Grace stares down at her hands in her lap. Although she claims to not mind talking about it, it's obviously difficult.

"The storm wasn't supposed to come ashore for another day. At least, that's what Benny told me before he left that afternoon. Dark clouds were already gathering on the horizon, and I begged him to wait. But he wouldn't listen. Thinking back, I suspect that he knew he'd be caught up in the weather, and could use it to further prove the seaworthiness of his invention. But it was so much worse than anyone anticipated. The largest storm ever recorded in our region.

"His boat was never found. We searched for days. Long after any hope remained and the coast guard called off the hunt, I still looked. But…Benny was just gone. Taken by the sea that he loved so much."

Ally sniffs next to Sam, and she turns to look sympathetically at her friend. As sad as the story is, though, Sam can't help but wiggle in her seat, distracted by the fact that she desperately needs to use the bathroom. They came straight from the school and she's been holding it since fifth period.

"Oh please, don't cry, dear." Grace snags some tissues from the coffee table and hands them to Ally. "That was six years ago. I'm really quite all right now, aside from becoming a bit of a recluse. After Benny's death, our close family friend, Gregory Kingsman, saved me from bankruptcy by salvaging the business. Since then, I've concentrated on overseeing the charities. I have no close family left since Benjamin and I never had children. I hate to be a cliché, but I'm afraid that's what I've become. The old widow all alone in the manor up on the hill, and all of that."

Laughing lightly at herself, Grace sets about arranging the items on the table, and then gives Ally another tissue.

"You're all alone here?" Cassy asks, leaning forward. The motion sets Sam's bladder into alarm mode.

Nodding, Grace makes her way to the impressive fireplace, and busies herself with putting another log on the fire. "It's how I want things. But I get out from time to time, for functions and such. It's kind of you to be concerned, but I assure you that I'm happy." It's a clear dismissal of the topic, and the perfect opportunity for Sam to speak up.

"I hate to ask, but do you possibly have a bathroom I can use?" While Sam is embarrassed to ask, she didn't actually think that their host would say no. However, it's clear that Grace is hesitating, paused with the fire poker in her hand.

"Ummm, of course!" she finally replies, turning towards the hallway. "Follow me."

Sam scrambles to keep up with the older woman, who is surprisingly quick. They go back to the foyer and then continue past it, down another, similar hall on the opposite side. Sam notes the tall ceilings and ornate trim work in the impressive home, all painted in rich creams and tans. Grace finally stops and opens the third door on their left.

"Here you go. Can you find your way back?"

The look Mrs. Potts gives her is in contradiction to her tone. Sam gets the distinct feeling that it's more of a warning, directing her not to wander. Which makes her curious.

"Sure I can. Thank you!" Ducking into the bathroom, Sam briefly wonders if it's possible for your bladder to explode.

A few short minutes later, she re-emerges in a much better state, half expecting Grace to be there waiting for her. The hall is empty, but as she turns towards the foyer, a distinct smell catches her attention.

Sniffing, Sam pauses, confused. It's a men's cologne. She's certain of it, because she and her mom spent hours scouring the stores this past Christmas looking for the distinct brand. Her mom first bought it for her dad three years ago and it's become harder to find each year. It's expensive, and her father only wears it on special occasions. Turning in the opposite direction, Sam follows the scent, which she is certain *wasn't* there when she entered the bathroom.

After turning a corner, the hallway opens up into a space that obviously serves as a mudroom. There's a built-in bench next to a backdoor. Rows of shoes line the floor opposite it, sitting under several jackets that hang from pegs. Another interior door to her left stands partway open, exposing steps leading down.

The cologne smell is already dissipating, and Sam feels the first pangs of guilt for not going straight back to the sitting room. But as she turns to go, she spots a pair of men's leather work boots, and freezes. They've been placed under a large black raincoat. What she finds fascinating about the clothing … are how both are glistening wet with fresh rain.

4

BENEFACTORS

"So, she likes to wear men's clothes when she works out in the garden," Ally says with a hint of frustration. "I don't understand why you won't let this drop."

Sam kicks at a rock littering the sidewalk, and considers her response. Their visit to the Potts' manor yesterday has been bugging her all day. "I told you, the boots were several sizes too large for her. Anyway, it's not so much the clothes, but the cologne. *Someone* must just walked through the hallway, and Mrs. Potts said she was alone."

"I'll bet she's not as alone as she likes everyone to think." Sam and Ally stop to look at Cassy, surprised by her statement. "Well, think about it," she continues, blushing slightly. Placing her hands on her hips, Cassy looks at her two friends with a hint of a mischievous smile. "Her husband has been gone for quite some time. It's not like she's that old, and I'm sure she must have *some* friends. Who's to say she doesn't have a boyfriend, and she was uncomfortable sharing that with a bunch kids she doesn't know?"

"Well, I think she's stunning, and it wouldn't surprise me at all," Ally agrees, looping one arm through Cassy's, and the other through Sam's.

The three of them continue down the sidewalk at a casual pace. Fortunately, Grace loved their idea and gave her blessing, so they're now on their way to the building that houses the afterschool program they're raising money for. It's a short distance from the middle school, and they plan to hit up the local stores in town for donations afterwards.

Sam can't think up any reason to disagree with Cassy and Ally, but she's come to rely on her intuition. She might not be able to say what it is that's bothering her about the situation at Mrs. Potts' house, but she *knows* that something is off.

Deciding to let it go for the time being, Sam

files the thought away for later examination. Squeezing Ally's arm, she then smiles at her. "Okay. You're right. I'll let it go. Do you think they'll let us talk to the kids that are there today, to see what they would want in the haunted house?" she continues, changing the subject.

Furrowing her eyebrows, Ally purses her lips at Sam. That was too easy. She knows her friend well and suspects this will come up again later.

"I still know most of the staff there," Cassy answers, unaware of the subtle exchange. "They're all really nice. I'm sure they'll be happy to talk with us about it!"

The three of them arrive at the building a few minutes later. It sits on the corner of the quaint, downtown area, an old house that was renovated into offices long ago. Cassy explained on the way there that the Potts purchased it for the afterschool program and made several needed upgrades. Looking at it now, Sam admires the rustic clapboard siding that matches the surrounding seaside theme. A slightly faded wooded sign over the main entrance reads, 'Ocean Side Afterschool Program' named for their small town.

A small bell over the door announces their arrival, and a young, dark-haired girl rushes out to greet them. "Hi, Cassy!" she cries, running around the small desk in the reception area. Although she's several years older than they are, Sam notices as they hug that Cassy is about the same height.

"Kim, these are my friends, Sam and Ally. We're helping to put together a haunted house at the middle school to raise money for the Potts' Foundation."

Kim steps back from Cassy and smiles even broader. "That's great!" Crossing her arms, she glances back down the hall she'd emerged from to make sure no one is there. "Because we could really use it," she continues, speaking much more quietly. Her smile gone, she reaches out to grasp Cassy's hand. "I overheard the director and Mr. Kingsman talking the other day. He was saying how he can't afford to give the program any more money, and we could be shut down before the end of this school year!"

"That's horrible!" Ally gasps.

"Hasn't this been here for a long time?" Sam questions, her mind working. "I know Lisa said you're struggling, but Mrs. Potts didn't mention anything about it being this serious."

Nodding her head vigorously, Kim turns her focus to Sam. "The Ocean Side Afterschool Program has been running for like, over ten years now. I started coming here when I was in third grade. I've been helping with the kids since last year, when I was a Junior. I've never heard anything about money trouble until last week. Mrs. Trent, the director, sounded really shocked, too."

"Kim, do we have some visitors?"

All four girls jump at the voice behind them, and turn as one to find an older, pleasant looking woman observing them. One eyebrow raised, she doesn't appear mad, as much curious.

"Mrs. Potts phoned and said you might be stopping by," she explains, coming forward to extend a hand to each of them. "I'm Mrs. Trent, the program director." She introduces herself before turning to Kim. "I need you back in the rec room, please," she instructs, a tight smile pulling at her lips.

Although Mrs. Trent doesn't say anything about the conversation, Sam is quite certain that she must have overheard at least part of it. Sam gets the distinct impression that Mrs. Trent will be having a private talk with Kim later about gossip.

Feeling guilty, even though she didn't have anything to do with the older girl divulging the private information, Sam fights not to blush too severely. Glancing at Ally, she notes that her red-headed friend is faring much worse, her cheeks burning a dark crimson.

"Cassy, I understand you attended our program for several years? I took over as the new director this past fall, so I don't think we ever met."

Sam is relieved to have the conversation steered away from finances. As Cassy and Mrs. Trent engage in a pleasant discussion, she takes a closer look around the room they're in.

While not fancy, the decorations are modern and tasteful, continuing with the sea theme. The walls are painted a light, seafoam green. The lower half is paneled with antique-looking bleached wood, giving the appearance of a picket fence. Someone was extremely clever and lined the top of it with an old anchor rope. Starfish, seashells, and even a small buoy hang from it at even intervals. Smiling at each new item, Sam turns in a complete circle to look at them all.

"Mrs. Potts has a knack for interior design."

Turning to Mrs. Trent, Sam is startled to find that everyone is staring at her. "Sorry," she apologizes, hoping the older woman doesn't think she's being rude for not being a part of the conversation. "I'm easily distracted."

Laughing, the director returns the smile. "I can relate. Here, you might find this interesting."

The three girls rush to keep pace, and follow Mrs. Trent to the far side of the room. They all stop in front of a large, highly polished, antique wooden ships wheel, positioned in the corner. It's the kind you see in pirate movies, where the captain stands at the helm, grabbing the spokes to steer the vessel.

Only this one has been turned into a memorial. Sam guesses that it's about as wide as she can spread her arms, and wonders what kind of ship it came from. The middle of it has been modified to hold a plaque, which includes a dedication and picture of the late Mr. Potts.

"To our friend and benefactor, Mr. Benjamin

'Benny' Potts. 12/10/1955 – 08/12/2010. May he rest in peace within the sea he loved so much. Dedicated by your friend, Mr. Gregory Kingsman." Ally reads the inscription aloud, and then turns to their guide. "Wasn't this school program the first one they founded?"

"Yes," Mrs. Trent confirms. "There are still nearly ten charities that the Potts' Foundation contributes to, but this afterschool program is the first and only one that was created and run solely by them. I was actually working in the office for Mr. Potts at his boat company when the … accident happened. Poor Mrs. Potts. I think it would have helped to some degree to have at least found the boat."

Sam reaches out and runs a hand softly over one of the spokes of the wheel, imaging what it must have been like, out there on the stormy water with his boat being torn apart. Shivering slightly, she pulls her hand away and focuses on the picture. Mr. Potts looked like a very pleasant man. With round cheeks and graying hair, he could have easily played Santa Claus by simply adding a beard. His blue eyes had a sparkle to them, the sort you find in people with a special flare for life. Sam knows instantly that he was someone she would have liked.

Just then, a group of rowdy kids burst from the hallway, Kim running close behind, trying to corral them. There are six of them, looking to be around eight years old, all dressed in various pirate outfits, complete with Styrofoam swords.

"Aye, matey!" a boy with an eye patch shouts. "Come back here! You have to go walk the plank!"

Shrieking, an even younger girl with a pirate hat on ducks out of his grasp and dashes behind Sam. "Okay, I surrender!" she hollers, feigning fear. "I'll take you to the shipwreck! I know where the gold is!"

Mrs. Trent just laughs, and before they know it, all three older girls are caught up in the play-acting. They're eventually led by sword point out into a backyard play area, where they are made to 'walk the plank'. Afterwards, they join all the kids for snack time and talk with them about what they want in the haunted house.

An hour later, the three friends reemerge from the charming building, full of conversation about the design they're rapidly coming up with.

They head back down the sidewalk, the local stores their new destination. They have a better idea now of what they'll ask for in donations.

Sam is distracted though, and only half-heartedly engaged in the conversation. She's bothered by a persistent thought gnawing at the back of her mind. Something about the pirates and a shipwreck. It brought up a distant memory that she's been struggling to remember. Her brother. Pirates. A secret cove containing a shipwreck.

Wait!

Stopping, Sam gasps at the revelation, and Cassy and Ally turn to look at her in surprise.

"What's wrong?" Ally asks, but already recognizes the look on her best friends face. She's seen it a number of times before and it causes a stir of excitement deep in her chest.

Looking at Cassy and Ally intently, Sam's eyes are wide. "I think I know where Mr. Potts' boat is!"

5

A PIRATE COVE

"I still don't understand *why* you think it's so important to go to the pirate cove," John states, glancing up in the rearview mirror. The three girls are crammed into the backseat of his small Honda Accord, with Sam sandwiched in the middle. His blue eyes lock briefly on her green ones, before focusing his attention back on the road. He's directing the question at her, since she was the one begging him this morning to take them on this excursion.

"You know how Sam is," Hunter says loudly around a mouthful of popcorn he brought for the journey. "She's got to turn everything into some sort of mysterious drama." Turning from his perch in the front seat, he tosses a handful of the snack at his younger sister's face.

Opening her mouth just in time to catch one of the kernels, Sam doesn't back away from her brother's criticism. "It's nothing like that." She moves her arm out of Cassy's way, so her friend can scoop up the rest of the popcorn from her lap. Constant hunger is a trait she shares with Hunter.

"I just think that if the old wreckage is Mr. Potts' boat, it would help give Mrs. Potts some closure. Besides, how many times did Ally and I beg you guys to let us go out there with you?" Sam crosses her arms and glares at the back of Hunter's head. Somehow sensing the scrutiny, he slides down in his seat without answering, and continues to dig noisily into the bag of food in his lap.

The pirate cove was a secret spot the two boys discovered three summers ago, while searching for a good place to fish. Nestled back in a dense area of trees that are partly submerged during unusually high tides, they found the remains of an old boat that was obviously in the water for a long time.

Sam recalls how excited the two were when they returned that afternoon, talking over each other, the possibilities growing with each telling. It was an ancient, lost ship, or part of a turn of the century passenger liner hauling riches across the ocean. Maybe it belonged to long lost explorers and there was a map somewhere in it that led to where they hid their gold.

Ally begged John for days to take them, but he insisted that it was too dangerous. That they had to forge treacherous waters to get there, and it was no place for kids. Of course, John was barely thirteen himself then, and once their parents got wind of the story, about a month later, it all came to a crashing halt.

Sam's parents took the boys to the local ranger station, where they then led the park official to the 'wreckage'. It ended up being on State land, an area that was part of one of many local state parks. Hunter and John had the proper fishing permits, and weren't doing anything wrong other than exaggerating their find.

According to Kathy Wolf, who explained the scene to Sam with a smile on her face, it was nothing more than a small section of a hull. The boys were messing with them yet again. The ranger estimated that it was less than twenty years old, and seeing as how garbage and relics from as far as Japan washed up often on the shores of the Pacific Northwest, he wasn't too interested in the find.

Hunter and John were a little sheepish for a few days, but they still refused to share their find with their younger sisters. Since it was too far for the young girls to explore on their own, the pirate cove maintained its secret, whimsical status. John and Hunter drifted apart that following school year, and no one has ever mentioned the place again. Until now.

"You do realize that the chance of this being Mr. Potts' boat is extremely slim."

John's voice breaks through Sam's daydreaming, and she jerks back to attention. The car has turned off the main road that leads south, out of town, and onto a less traveled graveled surface. They pass a small brown sign announcing the park entrance two miles ahead. There are several shortcuts and trails that kids on bikes can use to get to the park, but it's still an hour's ride. In the car, it's about half an hour.

Sam looks out at the water sparkling off to her right, part of Puget Sound. She tries to picture the stormy seas that occurred that night, tossing poor Mr. Potts around until his boat was torn apart. The sound is usually protected somewhat during storms, and not nearly as dangerous as out in the open waters, which is probably one of the reasons the seasoned seaman was caught off guard. *Could* part of his custom boat have been washed up here? Why not? It's certainly within what must have been the original search area. The sea could have held onto its loot for years though, before finally surrendering it during another, smaller storm.

"I know that," Sam finally answers, still staring at the water. "I just have a … feeling."

"Uh-oh," Ally moans, slapping a hand to her forehead. "I knew it!"

Cassy stops chewing and sits up straighter, her eyes brightening. "Really? Like, a legit *something isn't right* feeling? I knew it! What is it? Does it have to do with the whole cologne in the hallway thing, or the wet - "

"Whoa!" Sam hushes, cutting her friend off with a quick sideways glance to the boys. While

Cassy was an important part of their last mystery, she hasn't been involved in any of their other escapades. Sam gets that she's excited by the prospect, but they always have to be careful about how much they reveal to their brothers, or else risk endless teasing.

"Cologne?" Hunter echoes mockingly. "You better not be getting involved in anything," he warns, not even bothering to ask what it's about. "Mom will go ballistic."

"Don't worry about it." Sam leans forward, straining the seatbelt to its furthest length. Up ahead, the main park entrance is rapidly approaching, and she bounces slightly in the seat in her excitement. "Are we almost there?" she asks, intentionally changing the subject and not taking her brothers bait for a fight.

"Just about," John confirms with furrowed brows. He knows there's more to this, but decides to let it go. For now. "The parking area is right up here, but then we have a nice little hike. I hope we can remember where to go."

"I remember." Hunter lobs the empty bag of popcorn at Cassy playfully, who bats it aside. "Got a memory like a computer," he adds, tapping the side of his head.

"Yeah, maybe one that has a crashed hard drive," Sam counters. As the car comes to a stop, she climbs over a squealing Ally and leaps out the passenger door before her brother can grab her.

Running around to the driver's side, Sam then ducks behind John. He crouches down and extends his long arms out to either side. Laughing, Hunter lunges at the older boy unsuccessfully, giving up after a couple of tries.

"Just wait 'til I'm on varsity, Sam," Hunter says good-naturedly, holding his sides as if already winded. "I'll be four inches taller, and you won't be able to outrun me anymore!"

"I don't know about that, Hunter," Ally counters, leaning up against the car and watching the display with amusement. "I don't know anyone who can run as fast as Sam."

"Yeah," Cassy adds, jogging up to lightly side-tackle Hunter with a bump of her shoulder. "And you'd have to give up all the extra food."

Regaining his balance, Hunter turns to face Cassy, a very serious expression on his face. "You have a very valid point."

Peeking around John's solid form, Sam

laughs at her friends. Although it's well into Fall, it's an unseasonably warm day. The often-rainy skies are instead a crisp, bright blue. The sun has warmed the dry leaves on the ground, releasing a smell that Sam associates with jumping into leaf piles. It mingles with the rich scent of the towering pine trees that surround them, and Sam briefly wonders why they haven't come out here before, pirate cove or not.

Ally pushes away from the car, her bright red hair a stark contrast to the white vehicle. "Which way do we go?" she asks, eager to get underway.

"Ummmm…," Hunter mumbles, refocusing on his surroundings. Scanning the tree line along the parking lot, he spots an apparent bike trail, and wanders over to it. "This is the trail we used to get here," he explains, as everyone follows closely behind.

"Yup," John confirms. "It goes all the way to the trailhead at the city park, next to the cemetery."

"We would drop our bikes over here," Hunter continues, walking over to a paved footpath on the other side, next to a large sign with the park rules listed on it. "We'll go down this trail for a ways, and then there's a spot next to a big boulder where you turn off. That's the whole reason we found it, really. 'Cause we were climbing on the rock, trying to see who could get to the top of it first. John made it, and then spotted some water off through the trees. We figured that if we could find a secluded area to put our lines in, we might have a better chance of catching something, rather than at the public picnic and fishing area."

"Did you? Catch anything, I mean," Cassy asks, starting down the foot trail at a brisk pace.

"Nah. It's a horrible area to try and fish. No real beach or anything, since the trees pretty much extend out into the water."

With Cassy and the boys leading the way, Sam and Ally link arms and bring up the rear. It's cooler under the shade of the trees, and Sam is thankful for the sweatshirt she's wearing.

Before long, the group comes upon the described boulder and head off into the trees on an unmarked trail. After fifteen minutes of climbing over fallen logs, brushing aside branches, and avoiding stinging nettle, Sam isn't so sure that they're ever going to get there. Just as she's about to voice her concerns, John shouts from a ways ahead of them.

"We're here!"

Pushing through a large fern and nearly falling over a moss-covered rock, Sam finally stumbles into a large clearing. Her expectations having been built up over the years, her initial reaction is disappointment. Off to the far side of the open space, Hunter and John are standing atop an approximate five-foot long section of old boards, still loosely held together by a couple of cross-sections. The whole piece is smaller than a twin-sized bed, and aside from the aging wood, nothing else is left attached to it.

"That's it?" Ally murmurs, obviously also unimpressed.

"Well, we told you there was some exaggeration involved," John offers. "I said this would be a waste of time."

Undeterred, Sam moves closer to inspect the debris. They came all this way, and she's never been wrong before when following one of her hunches. Taking in the landscape, she quickly surmises how it even got here. Normally dry, like today, during extremely high tides, the woods in this area must fill with tidal water. It would have been a huge surge, to bring the remnants this far inland, leaving it behind when it retreated to the ocean.

Pulling her phone out of her back pocket, she snaps off a couple of pictures of the cove. Then, kneeling down next to the wood, she leans in close and reaches out to run a hand along the surface.

"Wanna magnifying glass, Sherlock?"

Cassy shoves at Hunter, who ducks out of the way.

Ignoring her brother, Sam scoots even closer, holding her phone up to get a clear shot of a single length of planking. Intrigued by her intense scrutiny, John and Ally also lean in.

"What is it, Sam?" Ally questions, only seeing old, weathered wood.

'This isn't wood," Sam answers slowly. Pushing back on her heels, she looks up at her best friend, a huge grin on her face. "And this *is* Mr. Potts' boat!"

6

THE GHOST OF EAGLE CREEK

Sam, Ally, and Cassy sit in a rough circle on the gym floor of Eagle Creek Middle School. Various department store bags are strewn around them, their donated contents spilling out. The result is what looks like a scene out of a Halloween story gone wrong. Masks, streamers, signs, plastic skeletons, and bags of cobwebs litter the floor, without any sort of obvious order.

Lisa Covington stands near the entrance to the gym, her hands resting on her slim hips as she watches the girls with a concerned expression. There were three other kids that originally showed up at their agreed upon meeting time of noon. However, they quickly found different excuses as to why they couldn't stay longer on a nice, Sunday afternoon. It's now three, and not much has been accomplished. Taking a deep breath, she tries to put on a positive appearance and approaches her sister and students.

"I'm afraid we're going to have to call it a day, girls."

"But we still have so much to do!" Sam gasps, alarmed at the how quickly the project is unraveling. Looking down at the map for the maze they're working on, she adds a line, creating another dead end where something scary can be placed.

"I'm sorry," Lisa continues, starting to gather up the decorations. "But I just got a call regarding the mare I looked at last week. They've selected Covington Ranch as her new home! Now Orion won't be alone. The only reason I can afford her is because she's a rescue horse, but she'll be perfect for the riding school once she's settled. I simply don't have time to go collect her during the school week, and they're limited on space and eager to get her placed. I have to leave soon, if I'm going to get her back home before dark."

While disappointed they have to cut their time short, Sam is excited by the prospect of a new horse! She and Ally have already made plans to work on the horse farm over the summer, so she'll be taking care of the mare. "What's her name?" Sam asks without a word of complaint while putting a scary clown mask in a bag.

"Glory," Lisa answers, pausing to turn and look at Sam. "Isn't that just the perfect name for a horse?"

"What if John and Hunter could come help us?"

Turning to Ally in surprise, Lisa tilts her head questioningly at her.

"I mean, John *is* sixteen," Ally implores. "Couldn't you trust him to lock up the gym after us? And he can give us a ride home."

"I heard Hunter say this morning that the two of them are just hanging out around the house today," Sam adds, her hopes rising.

"Don't you need help getting Glory?" Cassy asks her sister, torn between wanting to work on the project and meeting the new horse.

"The only time I'll need you is after I get her

back to the ranch," Lisa answers, still considering the proposal. "I suppose I could leave the keys with John, so long as you put everything away in the supply closet I showed you, and get back home by seven to help me."

Holding a hand up, Ally is already on her cell phone, speaking animatedly with her brother. "They'll be here in fifteen minutes!" she exclaims happily after hanging up. "But we *do* have a bag of candy here somewhere, right? Because there's bribery involved."

Laughing, Cassy digs around and quickly comes up with a large sack of assorted candy bars. "I think the cause justifies breaking into this."

Sam goes back to work on the diagram. Once it's done, they can start figuring out how to use the decorations, and how many pieces of cardboard they'll need.

Actually, she thinks to herself, *John and Hunter could be a big help with that.* Glancing over at a huge pile of large, flat panels of cardboard, Sam tries not to sigh. The whole thing is a little overwhelming. And she's trying not to think about the pirate cove and what they found. It was incredibly disappointing this morning, when Lisa told them that Mrs. Potts wasn't available to meet with them until tomorrow afternoon.

Touching the back pocket of her jeans briefly, Sam reassures herself that her cell phone is still there. On it are the pictures she took of the wreckage. She's convinced that it will bring Mrs. Potts the answer she's been waiting to get for six years.

Even though the boys aren't so sure, Sam believes that the odd material the planks are made of is the same experimental wood Mrs. Potts told them about. The one-of-a-kind boat that Mr. Benjamin Potts was taking on its maiden voyage that tragic day.

"Sam!" Lisa says loudly, pulling the young girl from her daydream. "I asked if you need anything before I leave," she repeats, laughing lightly at how high Sam jumped.

When Sam shakes her head, Lisa then hands her a small key. "This is to the supply closet. The one I pointed out to you, at the bottom of the stairs. Make sure that everything is picked up before you leave. The administration was adamant about that. They have basketball games in here again next Saturday, which is why we can't get back in to start setting the haunted house up until Sunday. Halloween is the following weekend. Do you really think it's going to be ready?"

"So long as we get more help and work on it during the week," Ally chimes in. "It's a good thing we're all doing well in our classes, and don't have too much homework."

"Yeah, we can do it!" Sam adds with more confidence than she feels, reminded of a test she still needs to study for. "It's going to be great!"

The boys arrive as Miss Covington is leaving, and they all spend the next three hours working hard. By six, the floor of the gym is covered in pieces of cardboard, laid out to mimic the drawing Sam made. They've carefully numbered them, so it can be quickly assembled on Halloween.

The panels all have creased edges, and are meant to stand up on their own. Lisa discovered them at a local business supply store. They're designed for large sales displays. Once up, they'll secure it all together with duct tape and then drape black plastic over the whole thing, to create the dark maze.

"This next week, we have to work on costumes and decorations." Sam makes the statement to no one in particular, as she stands staring at the work-in-progress.

"You're going to have to hit up your other club members for that," John replies. He starts stacking the cardboard in order by number. "Hunter and I have football practice every night after school."

Cassy lets out a big breath, blowing her bangs out of her eyes. "How did we end up being responsible for all of this?" she asks, kicking at a plastic rat with beady red eyes.

"Because it's going to be a huge success, and we'll make enough money to save the afterschool program," Ally assures her friend, gasping Cassy's hand and giving it a squeeze.

"Yeah, I'd love to stand around and sing a campfire song or something," Hunter jests, "but it's getting late. Mom's already texted me twice, and my stomach tells me that we're very late for dinner."

Already scooping things back into the bags, Sam throws a full one at her brother. "Then make yourself useful. All this stuff needs to go downstairs."

Within ten minutes, the five kids are loaded down with supplies, and gathered around the nondescript door at the back of the gym. There is no sign on it, only the letters, 'BR'.

"Boiler Room?" Ally guesses.

Sam's stomach does a little roll, and her heartbeat quickens. The early darkness of a fall night has already gathered around the school, and it suddenly seems more oppressive.

"The supply closet is down *there*?" Hunter's tone has changed from playful to tense.

"What's the matter, Hunter?" Sam pokes, as she slips the key in and unlocks the door. "Scared?"

Instead of answering, Hunter pushes past Sam and is the first to enter the dimly lit stairwell. Though he tries not to show it, he's obviously relieved to discover that the closet is located at the bottom, just two feet from the last step.

He's already got it open, and pulled the string attached to a lone, bare bulb which casts the space into swinging shadows.

"Is it all going to fit?" Cassy asks, poking her

head through the doorway.

"It's going to be tight," John agrees, stepping up next to Hunter. "Why don't you girls hand everything in to us, and we'll pack it in as best we can. Start with the cardboard."

After ten minutes of quietly feeding the stash into the small room, Sam finds herself at the back of the supply-line. Impatient and unwilling to stand still, her curiosity takes over and she wanders farther down the narrow hallway.

After about twenty feet, it branches off to the left and right, but both of those corridors are darker than the one she's standing in. About to turn back, a slight scuffling sound from somewhere in the murkiness stops her. Frozen with fear, the sound of her own heartbeat threatens to drown out any other noise and Sam forces herself to calm down.

There!

Spinning to her left, she squints into the gloom, trying to figure out what could be making the faint scraping noise.

"What is it?"

Nearly jumping out of her skin, Sam spins around to find Ally and Cassy standing right behind her. Laughing at herself, she grabs onto Ally's arms to keep from falling over.

"Oh my gosh! You nearly gave me a heart attack!" Stepping back, Sam points towards the faint sounds, which are rapidly fading away. "Footsteps!" she gasps, finally putting it together. "Like someone shuffling along with heavy boots or something."

"Why are we whispering?" John and Hunter have joined them, and the older boy is studying the hallway that Sam is still pointing down.

Sam didn't even realize she was whispering, and blushes slightly, knowing the boys will tease her endlessly about claiming to hear a ghost. But before she has a chance to admit to it, a louder, more resonating thud comes from farther away.

All five of them look at each other, wide-eyed. There's no mistaking the fact that they all heard the same thing, and that it came from somewhere in the basement. A space that is locked up, in a school that is supposed to be empty, except for them.

Without thinking, Sam begins to walk down the hall, but doesn't get far before a strong hand grabs her arm to stop her.

"What are you doing?" John demands, his face a mask of concern.

"There has to be an explanation," Sam says reasonably. "Maybe somebody left an outside door open and it caught in the wind. We were left with the responsibility to make sure the school is locked up, so we should check. I would hate to have Lisa get in trouble because of it."

"Or we can call Lisa and have her come back," Cassy offers, obviously not interested in investigating the sound.

"She won't be able to," Ally states. "She's probably got the horse loaded up by now and is just starting on her way back. Remember? She's in another town. I agree with Sam. Let's just take a quick look. If we hear anything else, we can call my dad."

Sam's surprised at her friend's bravery. While she's never backed down from a mystery, it's often because of Sam's prompting and convincing, not the other way around.

"I guess," John starts, and the slight loosening of his hand is all Sam needs. Pulling away, she quickly starts back down the hallway, leaving her friends the choice to either follow or stay behind. They all follow.

At the next juncture, another fifty feet away, a red sign with an arrow points to the right. Under it are the initials 'BR' again. Sam follows it without hesitation.

After only taking a couple of steps though, she pauses, raising her nose to the stale air and breathing deeply. The hairs once again begin to prickle on the back of her neck. It's the same cologne she smelled the other day in Mrs. Potts' house!

Ally pushes up into her back, grasping her around the waist. "What is it?" she whispers in her ear, sensing the tension.

Without answering, Sam shakes her head in response, and then the five creep forward as a group. There's an electricity in the air, and it isn't clear whether it's the artifact of a soul that met a sudden death, or merely the work of their imaginations.

The hall eventually opens up into a large room, the ceiling lined with bare pipes. On the far end is a steel cage, housing what looks like a large, cast iron monstrosity. As they grow closer to it, the same banging they heard before explodes in the room, causing them all to jump, and Cassy to scream!

Spinning as one towards the source, John is the first to point out the newer-looking heating unit. It's housed in a similar-looking cyclone-like fencing, but the large gate on the front of it is open. As they watch, the humming coming from the machine cuts off and the gate again swings slightly, banging in its frame.

"The janitor must have left that open," John guesses. "As it got dark out, the temperature dipped enough to kick the furnace on, and the backdraft from its intake as it shuts on and off is enough to move that gate."

Laughing, Cassy smacks Hunter on the back. "You really thought there was a ghost, didn't you?"

Sam doesn't pay attention to her brother's response, as she makes her way over to a plaque that's situated on the wall, next to what has to be the boiler. The smell of cologne is stronger here, and she's almost not surprised when she recognizes the face of the man on the memorial.

It reads:

TARA ELLIS

In memoriam of a friend and beloved employee of Eagle Creek Middle School.
May his soul rest in peace.
1939 – 1969.
Thaddeus B Potts.

7

FAMILY TIES

"I heard something else *before* the banging," Sam insists, pushing aside a branch. She's talking to both Ally and Cassy, who are following close behind her. They started their trek up the hill to Mrs. Potts' house as soon as class let out. Sam's discovery the night before made sitting through the day even harder. Now, not only does she have the pictures of the wreck to share with her, but a ton of questions about the obvious family connection between Benjamin Potts and the janitor that is supposed to be haunting the halls of Eagle Creek Middle School.

Cassy spotted a trail that looked well-used part way up the long, paved road, so they opted to follow it. Since the Potts' house is the only one at the top, it makes sense that this is a short cut.

A large crack of thunder rips through the sky above them, and Sam pauses to look up. The skies nearest them are still blue, but they spotted the dark clouds out over the ocean before entering the trees. Picking up the pace, she continues her train of thought.

"It sounded like footsteps. And it was moving *away* from us. I'm telling you, I think there was someone else down there."

"Then why didn't you say something to the boys?" Ally scolds, always the one to think of safety first. It was the reason Sam didn't tell her best friend until now.

"Because it's obvious that whoever it was, didn't want to be found," Sam reasons, stepping over a large root. "I didn't think we were in any danger," she adds for Ally's benefit. The trail is steeper than she thought it would be, and she's beginning to get winded.

"Or maybe we have two different ghosts, wearing the same cologne?" Cassy suggests, referencing the fragrance Sam previously mentioned. Cassy didn't notice it last night, but

Ally had caught a whiff of it.

Sam smiles at her friend's clever joke, but it troubles her that she doesn't have a good comeback. Frowning now, she's relieved to see the familiar driveway up ahead through the trees. The first drops of rain are just starting to fall.

They climb the impressive front steps, and Sam barely has a chance to drop the elaborate knocker a second time, when the door is yanked open by Mrs. Potts. She smiles warmly at them, in stark contrast to their first greeting a few days ago.

"Girls! It's so great to see you. Hurry up and come inside, before this storm unleashes on you!"

Happy to oblige, the three friends rush inside and kick their sneakers off in the foyer. Once again, a welcoming fire is popping and snapping in the sitting room.

"Thanks for agreeing to see us, Mrs. Potts," Ally says, hanging her damp windbreaker on a vacant hook.

"Please, do call me Grace. I don't have many friends, so I'd rather keep things informal!"

Sam smiles at the older woman, happy that

she would call them her friends. Today, she is dressed more casually in a stylish, yellow jogging outfit. Her hair is tied up with a matching yellow scrunchie, and Sam thinks how the bright color makes her face appear more youthful.

"Sam," Grace says over her shoulder as she leads the way into the warm sitting room. "You sounded rather eager on the telephone. I apologize for not being available this weekend, but my schedule was much busier than usual. There was a fundraising banquet on Saturday evening, and then a rotary club meeting yesterday afternoon, after church. What is it you need to talk with me about?"

Now that she's seated in front of Mrs. Potts, Sam feels a sudden sense of unease. What if the discovery of the boat has the opposite effect Sam expects? What if she is heartbroken, rather than comforted? Glancing nervously at her friends, Sam notes that they are seated in the exact same spots as before, with her sandwiched between Ally and Cassy on the loveseat, even though there is another empty one across from them. The familiar setting helps to settle her nerves and when she spots a pitcher of lemonade and plate of cookies set out on the old wood coffee table, she is further encouraged. Mrs. Potts really is happy to have them there.

"Mrs. – I mean, Grace," Sam begins, quick to correct herself. "When we were putting away our decorations last night at the school, we happened to see a memorial." While eager to show the photos to their host, Sam figures she'll start with the easier of the two topics.

"Oh, yes!" Grace exclaims, nodding her head. "Thaddeus Potts. I'm sure you must have figured out the family relation, based on the name."

"And from the picture," Cassy adds. When Grace gives her a questioning look, she rushes to explain. "We stopped by the afterschool program on Friday, and saw the cool ship wheel plaque for your husband. His picture is on it, and he looks *just* like Thaddeus Potts!"

"That's because Thaddeus was Benjamin's father," Grace states, picking up the plate of cookies. Passing them to the girls, she then pours herself a cup of lemonade. "I picked the pictures out for both of those dedications," she continues, a faraway look in her eyes. "Although Thaddeus died when Benny was just fifteen, it was a full thirty years later before his devotion to the school was recognized. Our rotary donated it.

"I was rather put out when I heard that it was placed in the *basement*. I expected it to go in the front hall. However, Benny was adamant that I not make a fuss over it, and thought that it was rather appropriate it be in the space his father spent the most time in."

Sam digests this information, while accepting a cool glass of juice to help chase the cookie she's munching. "I don't know a good way to ask this, but according to my brother, there's a ghost story surrounding the … accident that he died in."

To Sam's surprise, Mrs. Potts chuckles and claps her hands together. "You mean the boiler explosion? That story has been exaggerated with each telling! While there *was* a small steam leak that caused the original injury, Thaddeus in no way died in that building."

"I knew it!" Cassy shouts, in spite of her mouth being full of cookie.

"What really happened, then?" The more rational Ally asks, scooting forward.

"Thaddeus suffered a moderate steam burn to a good portion of his arm," Grace explains.

"He would have been perfectly alright, but he was a stubborn man, much like my Benny. He refused medical care, and it ended up becoming infected. By the time he was talked into going to the hospital, he was septic. That's where the infection reaches your bloodstream, and causes your internal organs not to work properly. Medical treatment in 1969 in a small town wasn't very aggressive, and when they finally transferred him to a larger facility, it was too late. He never recovered from it, and Benny was fatherless at the age of fifteen.

"He used to spend hours in that basement with his father, Thaddeus. As a janitor, he was needed for other matters on the grounds during the day, while the children were present. In the afternoon, he would go down to the basement and make the rounds, checking to insure that the aging boiler system was working properly. Benny told me how proud he was the first time his mother allowed him to walk the trail over to the school, and spend the afternoon with his dad. They had a very modest home at the base of this hill. Even after he entered high school, Benny would still join his father when he could. It was a special time together for them. It was because of that experience, that he became the man I fell in love with. With the same dedication to hard work as his father, he did the one thing Thaddeus fell short of: chasing his dreams. *That* is what led to the Potts' Boat Company."

Seizing the mention of Benjamin Potts and his boat store, Sam tentatively takes her phone from her back pocket. She quickly pulls up the first picture from the cove, and shoves it in Grace's direction before she loses her nerve.

"What's this?" the older woman asks, taking the phone and looking closely at the image.

"I think it might be the remains of Mr. Potts' boat," Sam answers, practically whispering. Without any further explanation, she moves over to sit next to Grace, and swipes her finger across the surface of her phone until the close-up shot of the plank is visible.

Clearly stunned, Grace stares at the image for a full two minutes before letting out a pent up breath. "Where did you find this?" Her emotions are hard to read, but she looks up at Sam and there is an intensity in her grey eyes that wasn't there before.

"In a hidden cove out in the state park south of town," Sam replies, afraid to look away. "Our brothers found it several years ago. They bragged about it, calling it the pirate cove, but never told us where it was. After visiting the afterschool program Friday, I suspected it could be your husbands boat. When I saw the unusual material used to make the planks, I figured it might be Mr. Potts' invention." Her heart nearly in her throat, Sam rushes through her explanation in one breath, afraid of the reaction it was going to cause.

Finally closing her eyes and breaking the contact, Grace nods her head slowly. Handing the phone out to Sam, she again looks at her, this time with an obvious amount of respect. "I believe you are right. You've managed to solve a six-year mystery in a matter of days."

Blushing furiously, Sam suffers an odd mixture of relief and anxiety. She wasn't exactly sure what kind of reaction she expected, but this certainly wasn't it. Confused, she takes the offered phone back, and tries to figure out how to respond.

"We're sorry if this is upsetting," Ally offers,

saving Sam from the awkward moment. "We thought it might help in some small way, to finally find the wreckage."

"My dear, you have nothing to apologize for," Grace says, visibly putting her emotions in check. Sitting up straighter on the lounge, she tugs at the hem of her shirt, as if pulling out the wrinkles will further convince them of her strength.

"Quite the contrary. I am impressed with you all, and this discovery *does* help. It really does. In ways you can't imagine."

The statement ads another layer of mystery to the ones already rolling around in Sam's head, and she looks questioningly at Grace. What could she possibly mean by that?

"I do have a favor to ask of you all, though." Standing, Grace walks to the mantle, and then turns to stare out the large windows that line the wall behind them. The storm has progressed outside, and rain whips at the glass, tapping out a song of random chorus.

"If you haven't already shared this with anyone, I would prefer that we keep the discovery quiet for now. I'm afraid that the news would bring … unwanted attention. I've been at a bit of odds with Mr. Kingsman," she confides, looking away from the view outside and back at the girls seated in front of her. "We don't agree on how he practices business, and I've rather enjoyed not having to deal with him lately. This would not only cause all sorts of media exposure for me, but it would undoubtedly force me back into a confrontation with Gregory."

This declaration produces an explosion of questions that forces Sam to bite down on her lip to prevent herself from asking them. Now isn't the time. Mrs. Potts is clearly having a hard time talking about it, and pressing her for more information would not only be rude, but could possibly cause a rift in their new friendship.

"Our brothers are the only other people that know," Sam confides. "But don't worry, they don't believe me anyway, and they won't say anything if we ask them not to."

"I would never suggest that you keep something from your parents," Grace says, going back to sit beside Sam. "I didn't mean that I want to you to keep a secret, only that it not be shared with the media, or anyone that doesn't need to know."

"Of course!" Cassy adds. "We understand. We would never go to the media! This is your information to do with what you want. We just wanted to try and help."

"And you have!" Grace then turns and starts cleaning up the remnants of their snack, a sign that perhaps they've reached the end of their visit.

Looking outside, Sam discovers the rain has let up considerably. "We should probably get going," she states, helping to brush some crumbs off the table and onto the plate. "It looks like the storm has passed."

"Do keep me updated on the progress of the haunted house." Walking from the room, the three girls glance at each other before following Grace out to the foyer.

Once there, Sam suddenly realizes that with all her worry over the revelation of the boat, she was forgetting one of her other goals. Feeling a twinge of guilt, she turns to Grace, instead of putting her shoes on. "Do you think I could have a small glass of water before we go? I probably shouldn't have eaten that last cookie," she adds, almost hoping that her ploy to see further into the mysterious house will fail.

Hesitating only briefly, Grace smiles warmly at Sam. "Of course you can! Follow me."

Leaving Ally and Cassy to finish putting their shoes and jackets on, Sam scoots through the same hallway she explored before. Not knowing what she's looking for, she keeps an eye out for anything odd or out of order. In her limited experience with clues, Sam has learned they often present themselves when you least expect it. Noting that she doesn't detect any cologne this time, she continues moving forward.

Stepping through the mud room (this time vacant of any men's boots or raincoat), she emerges into a large, bright kitchen. True to the style of the rest of the house, everything is grand and meticulous. Other than some dishes in the big double sink, it's spotless.

Mrs. Potts grabs a glass from a cupboard and fills it from the tap. Going to stand next to her, Sam can't help but glance at the items in the sink: two small plates, two forks, and two teacups.

The implication doesn't sink in until she's halfway through her drink, and Sam nearly chokes. *Two* of everything!

Seeming to notice Sam's wide-eyed expression, Grace steps in front of her, and begins to busy herself with loading the dishes into the dishwasher. Suddenly noticeably anxious, she starts rambling about how she was so busy the past couple of days that she was falling behind on her housework.

Reaching to set the now empty glass on the counter, Sam is about to comment on how much cleaner her house is than theirs, when she glances at the open dishwasher. Sitting on the bottom rack are two bowls, and two large dinner plates. In the utensil rack are two spoons and two forks.

Unless ghosts are into sitting down to a meal, Sam thinks, backing away and crossing her arms across her chest, *it would seem that Mrs. Potts doesn't live alone!*

8

MOUNTING CLUES

The rest of the week crawls by. Sam has a hard time concentrating on math and science when all she can think about is what to paint on the walls of the haunted house, and what the clues at the Potts' estate mean.

Cassy and Ally aren't convinced that they mean *anything*, and maintain the belief that Grace simply prefers her privacy. Sam considers discussing it with Lisa, but decides that it feels too much like gossip. Instead, she focuses on recruiting more help for Halloween night, and succeeds in finding four other kids to act as characters inside the haunted house.

The club meets twice after school during the

week, but is forced to use the library since the gym is tied up every night for sports. They come up with a plan for a paint party on Sunday. The boys even seem interested in helping more, and Sam is feeling encouraged that they might actually pull it off.

Friday finally rolls around, and Sam, Ally, and Cassy file onto the bus together, laughing and making plans to have a sleepover. They eventually settle on Ally's house, because her Mom has a rare night off, and has offered to supply pizza and movies. She's an Intensive Care nurse at the nearest hospital, and normally works overnight shifts on the weekend. In all the years they've been friends, Sam still doesn't feel like she really knows Mrs. Parker, they've spent such little time together. She's looking forward to what should be a fun night!

The bus rumbles through the small town of Ocean Side, making frequent stops. They used to be able to walk to the elementary school, but the middle school is too far, and it would still take them close to half an hour to reach on bikes. Sam is daydreaming about the time when they'll finally be at the more centralized high school, when she can't help but notice a very large, new billboard sign set along the side of the main road.

Staring out at her with dark, serious eyes is a middle-aged man in a business suit. His head is cocked to one side, with an 'I-told-you-so' expression on his face. Below his crossed arms are large, bold words:

I'M THE MAN YOU NEED IN OFFICE
VOTE
GREGORY KINGSMAN
Your next Washington State Congressman

Turning her head to watch the sign shrink behind them, Sam wonders about the man in the advertisement. Grace certainly doesn't like him. *What did she say about him?* Sam taps at her chin, trying to remember. *That they didn't agree on how he practices business. And Kingsman is the one who bought out the boat company after Mr. Potts died.*

Settling back into the hard bench seat, Sam is vaguely aware of the animated conversation Cassy and Ally are having beside her. Glancing at the girls, she catches movement beyond them, and looks around to see a young boy of about eight waving at her from a seat across the aisle. She recognizes him from the afternoon school program. She believes he was the pirate who made her walk the plank into the ball pit. Smiling, she waves back, and is reminded of the dire situation that the charity is in.

Business practice, Sam repeats to herself, staring down at her hands now. *The teen helping out at the program said it was a shock to find out they were in financial trouble, and the news came from Gregory Kingsman!*

"What are you thinking about, Sam?"

Sam jerks her head around at Ally's question, and then blushes when she finds that both of her friends are staring at her.

"I'm thinking that it's time we did a little snooping."

***

"Move aside," Cassy orders. Tossing her half-eaten piece of pizza back onto a paper plate, she shoos Sam off the office chair, and slides in front of the Parkers' computer. "Let me have a shot at it." Cracking her knuckles dramatically, she begins tapping at the keyboard.

They're gathered at one end of a large rec room, the most kid-friendly area of Ally and John's impressive house. It's nearly ten at night and they just finished watching a movie on the large flat screen TV with Ally's parents. While Sam enjoyed the time, and getting to know Brandon and Elizabeth Parker better, she was itching to start looking for information. It was with a mingled sense of guilt and relief that she told them goodnight just a few minutes ago.

Watching over Cassy's shoulder, Sam is impressed with the different ways she's coming up with to search for Gregory Kingsman. All Sam found were information pieces on his political campaign. After a few creative inputs, Cassy was stacking up pages of past articles on various topics.

Sam was encouraged earlier when her friends agreed to try to connect some of the dots. She just *knows* there is something questionable going on with Mrs. Potts, Kingsman, the afterschool program, and the boat company. And it all goes back to the disappearance of Mr. Potts.

Pausing, Sam considers her use of the word disappearance, instead of death.

"A body was never found," She says aloud without realizing it.

"What do you mean?" Ally looks at Sam for an answer, her normally pleasant face appearing rather alarmed.

"Mr. Potts was never found, and was *presumed* dead," Sam explains. "But what if he wasn't?"

Cassy pivots the chair around to face Sam. "Why would he hide? What would be the point? And poor Mrs. Potts. I can't imagine him doing that to her."

"Their business was going bankrupt," Sam answers slowly, thinking things through as she says it. "Remember? Grace said that Mr. Kingsman saved it by bailing it out after Mr. Potts' death. But something obviously happened since then, to make her distrust the man. There has to be more," she continues, running her hands through her hair and staring up at the ceiling. "I wonder," Sam continues, still more to herself than anyone else, "If Mr. Potts had a large life insurance policy. And … if he prefers a certain pricey cologne."

"Sam!" Ally gasps, alarmed. "How could you suspect such a horrible thing of Grace? Do you really think she would *lie* about her husband's death? I agree that there's some odd stuff going on, but that's a stretch."

Before Sam has a chance to defend herself, the doors to the rec room burst open and John and Hunter make a loud entrance.

"What's the heated discussion all about?" John asks, looking from his sister and back to Sam. It's unusual for the two girls to disagree so strongly, and Sam can see the concern etched into the lines of his dirty face.

They had a football game tonight, and they're still wearing their sweaty gear. John's jersey is notably marked with the colors of the opposing team, while Hunter's is nearly clean. As a junior at the high school, John is on the varsity team, but Hunter is just a freshman and it's his first year playing. It would be unusual for him to do anything on a Friday night, other than warm the bench.

The girls normally go to the games, but with another wet and chilly evening predicted, they chose the dryer option of movies and pizza, instead.

Sam quickly brings the boys up to speed on the investigation, filling them in on the details they were keeping from them. At this point, she figures they can use all the help they can get.

"Ally, please don't be upset with me." Now that Sam has recapped everything that's happened over the past couple of weeks, she's more certain than ever that her hunch is right. "I like Grace as much as you do, and I'm sure that if I'm right, that she has a good explanation for it."

"Well, this Gregory Kingsman guy *does* seem a little shady," Cassy interrupts, pulling up one of the first articles she found. "This one is from fifteen years ago, before he was even into politics. Says he was indicted for illegal trading on the stock market. But ... " Cassy scans over the rest of the publication. "He was never charged. I'm guessing he used the money to buy his first company, which is what *this* article is about." Clicking on the next tab, she reads the title aloud. "Previous resident, Gregory Kingsman, returns to Ocean Side and purchases local business."

"Which one?" Hunter asks, already on his third piece of cold pizza.

Sam wrinkles her nose at the combined smell of pepperoni and body odor. The guys really need to go take a shower.

"The restaurant on the marina," Cassy answers. "You know the really fancy one that always has fresh crab and lobster? I've never actually eaten there, just stared at the tank full of lobster in the lobby."

"We go there on special occasions," Ally says, nodding her head. "But I don't think he owns it anymore. My mom knows the owners, and it definitely *isn't* him."

"Well, I guess that isn't surprising." Cassy continues to click through the other records, most of them about his continuous purchases and sales of various types of businesses. "Looks like he got into politics about ten years ago, and the Potts used to be big supporters. And here is the one about the boating accident," she continues, more subdued. "Mr. Kingsman launched his own private search party, too. And then there's a whole piece here about how he saved Mrs. Potts from losing everything, by salvaging the failing boat business." Cassy reads that one out loud in its entirety.

Sam's frown deepens as they learn that while Mrs. Potts still maintains a connection as a limited silent partner, Kingsman is now the majority shareholder and owner. In exchange for the bailout, Grace gave up all control, and any money she makes goes to the charity organizations.

"It sounds like he really helped her out," John says a little reluctantly. "Why do you think she's opposed to him now?"

"What's the name of Boat Company now?" Sam asks, looking over Cassy's shoulder again. Together, they go over the whole article, but don't see it mentioned anywhere.

"Hold on!" Ally shouts, and sprints from the room. A minute later, she returns holding an open phonebook. Running her finger down the page, she finds what she's looking for. "Kingsman Custom Boating Supplies."

Sitting down next to Cassy, Sam enters the name and is rewarded with an instant result. A professionally designed webpage displays the most popular products under an elaborate banner, which includes the same picture of Gregory Kingsman that was on the billboard.

"I'm already getting sick of seeing that fake smile," Ally complains.

Sam hopes it's a sign that Ally is starting to come around, and she turns a curious eye to the first item on the page. There are bold, red words flashing 'Best Seller' above it and Sam clicks onto the icon. The page is then filled with a large image that practically takes Sam's breath away.

"Hey!" Hunter shouts, pausing midway through his fourth piece of pizza. "Isn't that your mystery wood from the Pirate Cove?"

"Yes," Sam mumbles, leaning close to the monitor. There is little doubt that the 'unique and unbreakable wood' advertised as the Kingsman Custom Boating Supplies bestseller, is none other than Mr. Potts' invention. Smaller lettering details that it was first introduced five years ago, one year after Benjamin Potts' disappearance.

"I wonder," Sam says to her friends that have all crowded in close behind her to get a better look, "If the noises in the basement feeding the current ghost stories started about six years ago."

A moment of uneasiness passes as they all look at each other, wanting to dispute the possibility but unable to come up with a reasonable argument against it. Could it be, that after faking his own death, Benjamin Potts began returning to the one place he felt safe as a child?

Sam is the first to break the silence.

"Who's up for some ghost hunting?"

9

HOW TO CATCH A GHOST

By Sunday evening, Sam is so wound up that she can hardly concentrate on painting. They have a great turnout, which includes the three students that originally signed up for the club, and the four others Sam recruited earlier in the week. With the additional help of Hunter and John, they already have all of the panels decorated before the end of the day.

Sam's main concern is how to orchestrate a repeat of last Sunday, with just the five of them left alone in the building. This is critical to their plan working. She would never lie to Lisa, but Sam knows that if she were to tell her what's going on, Lisa would shut them down. She might be more open to mysteries than most adults, but Lisa understands how Sam's parents feel about it.

Sam's learned a lot this past year about communicating better with her mom and dad, but she doesn't feel like they have crossed into territory yet where they're doing anything wrong. It could very well be that there isn't anything, or *anyone* in the basement and it's all been a big coincidence. Once they're sure, then they'll actually *have* something to tell an adult.

Fortunately, what seems to be a typical scenario develops and all the other kids have reasons why they have to leave before it's time to pick up. Various jars of poster board paint are strewn around the gym floor, with corresponding paper plates and paint-filled paintbrushes. The cardboard panels are still drying, and while it all looks amazing, there's a lot of work to do before they're done for the evening.

"Goodness!" Lisa Covington exclaims, glancing at her watch. "It's nearly six and we're nowhere close to being done. It's a good thing we ordered the pizza, but I don't know how much longer I can stay. The horses need tending before it gets dark."

"I can stay and lock up again," John offers.

Sam feels a wave of relief as Lisa happily agrees, and gives him the keys. She can see a certain amount of guilt on John's face, though, and hopes he doesn't feel badly. It's exactly how he would have reacted, even if they didn't have an ulterior motive.

By seven, the kids have the mess picked up, and the boards are dry enough to stack. They work in silence, each lost in their own thoughts as to what they might find under the school.

Once they make their way down the shadowy stairs, they go out of their way to talk loudly to each other. Sam's laughter echoes back at her when she overreacts to a stupid joke that Hunter tells. John opens the supply closet door a little too hard, so that it slams back against the wall, reverberating loudly. Cassy squeals as Hunter chases her with a still damp paintbrush, and Ally yells at him to stop.

Perfect.

Sam bounces on the balls of her feet, impatient to be done. Glancing up and down the hallway, she hands another panel in to John and then breathes a sigh of relief when she realizes it's the last one. Time for the next phase!

"Come one!" she shouts. "It's getting really late. Mom is going to be wondering where we are, and I've still got homework to do!"

"So do I," Cassy answers from the top of the stairs. "I seriously need to study for a math test, too, or I'm afraid I might fail it."

They all make a show of talking and stomping up the stairs, but then sneak quietly back down and into the supply closet. Ally is eventually the last one at the top. Once alone, she slams the door, waits a few minutes, and creeps very slowly back to her friends. Cassy's idea that Ally was the smallest, and therefore the less likely to make any noise, was a good one.

The next ten minutes feel like forever, as they huddle in the pitch-darkness of the supply closet. Unfortunately, Sam was the first in, and she's smashed up against the back wall, Hunters elbow pushing painfully into her shoulder blade.

Sam is beginning to wonder if poster board paint fumes can make you sick, especially when mixed with smelly teen boys, when John finally eases the door open. Dim lights that are always on in the subterranean hallway seep inside, casting them all into shadows.

"It looks clear," John whispers before pushing the door all the way open.

Doing their best to step lightly, the five kids file out into what now feels like a forbidden place. Somehow, having the door at the top of stairs closed makes every dark corner and unknown noise more sinister.

Motioning soundlessly, Sam waves Hunter, Cassy, and Ally to begin their assigned search, while she and John go the opposite direction, towards the boiler room. They figure it will increase their odds of corralling the 'ghost' if they split up. The outermost hallway makes one big loop, so they'll eventually meet up again at some point if they don't stop.

After going no more than fifty feet, John suddenly freezes in front of Sam, causing her to run into his back. Too scared to even rub at the bump on her forehead, she instead grabs onto his nearest arm.

"What is it?" she gasps, trying to see the far end of the hall.

"Shhh." Holding a hand up to further emphasize his demand for silence, John tips his head to the side, obviously listening.

There!

Sam hears it, too. The same odd shuffling sound from last week! They turn and stare at each other, wide-eyed.

Continuing to move stealthily forward, they inch their way down the corridor, the noises getting louder and more defined. Reaching the next bend it becomes clear that whoever it is, they're definitely in the boiler room.

Sam doesn't even realize that she's still got an iron grip on John's arm, until she has to pry her fingers free to pull out her cell phone. Tapping out a message to Ally, she instructs them to continue until they reach the boiler room, on the opposite side of the large room. That way, whoever it is will *have* to go past one of the groups in order to leave. There's an outside door, but it's on the far side of the building, accessible only by this main hall.

Sam and John flatten themselves against the wall near the entrance to the room, listening to the sounds that are now more distinct. Her heartrate slowing slightly as she admits to herself that it's clearly a person moving about and not a ghost, Sam almost wishes that she was wrong.

Directly across from them, Hunter peeks his head out and nods to indicate that they are all in position. Sam feels John go rigid as he takes a deep breath and steels himself for a possible confrontation. Fumbling with her phone, she dials 91, and hovers with her finger over the last single digit, just in case.

"Hello!" John's voice booms, and the effect is immediate. The noises stop, and a sudden heaviness fills the space, like a pent up breath waiting to explode. "We know that someone is down here. You need to identify yourself, or else we'll call the police!"

An odd sort of wheezing sound answers him and Sam sees a wave of fear cross her brothers face as he stars back at them in horror. She figures he's imaging a burned, disfigured ghost making the sounds, and suppresses a shudder.

"I mean it! You're trespassing, and we'll call the cops!" John's voice has lost some of its conviction, however, and he motions to her to finish dialing.

Hesitating, Sam is about to do as ordered when she notices a familiar scent, and then there's a banging sound, followed by a cry of pain from an older man.

"Mr. Potts?" she cries out impulsively. Stepping around John before he has a chance to stop her, Sam stumbles forward into the room. "Please don't be afraid! My name is Samantha Wolf. I'm friends with your wife, Grace!"

Standing only ten feet away from her is a thin, pale man with a shock of grey hair. His face is so gaunt that she barely recognizes him from his picture. He's fallen over a toolbox left out on the floor, and is looking up at her with watery blue eyes.

"Please don't call the police," he begs, his voice weak and hoarse.

Without another thought, Sam rushes forward to help the ghost of Eagle Creek Middle School.

10

PHANTOM SECRETS

"Do you need us to call an ambulance?"

Sam looks back at Ally, glad that her friend asked the question. She's helped the ailing Mr. Potts up into a sitting position, but he looks horrible. Beads of sweat line his pale forehead, even though the room is cool enough for sweatshirts, and his breathing is ragged.

Shaking his head, the older man mumbles something indistinguishable. But when Ally takes her phone out to make the call, he suddenly straightens up.

"No!"

Although weak, the word is clear, and Ally hesitates.

"Mr. Potts," John tries, dragging a chair over to him. "I really think you should get to a hospital, sir." Mr. Potts begrudgingly allows John to help him onto the chair.

Sam rocks back on her heels and gazes up at the man that was supposed to have been dead for the past six years. She can't help but feel horrible. It was because they gave the man such a scare, that he fell. Granted, it looks like he was already sick, but it couldn't have helped.

"No," Mr. Potts repeats, more clearly this time. "Please. I don't need an ambulance. Just give me a few minutes to catch my breath, and I'll be fine."

Sam looks to John, who gives a little nod. Relief washes over her, and she desperately wants to believe that he really will be okay. John's been through advanced first aid training while in the Scouts program, and she trusts his judgement. Standing, she turns to Cassy. "Can you go find him a drink of water?" she asks.

"I'll go with you," Hunter volunteers, and the two of them rush from the room on the mission, glad to have something to do.

"Here," Ally says softly. Pulling her jacket

off, she wads it up and places it behind his lower back to provide some cushion against the cold metal chair. Moving next to Sam, she pushes some of her unruly red hair out of her face and looks nervously at her. It's clear that Ally is feeling just as guilty. Widening her eyes in a 'what now' gesture at Sam, she then takes a deep breath and slowly releases it before asking the question they're afraid of knowing the answer to. "Did you hurt anything when you fell?"

"You mean other than my pride?"

It takes a moment for the joke to break through the tension in the room, but when it does, they all laugh thankfully at the change in the atmosphere.

"We're sorry if we startled you," Sam offers. "But we weren't certain who was down here, and we had to make sure."

Waving a hand at her, Mr. Potts leans back in the seat. "No apologies needed, young lady. In fact, *I'm* the only one here that owes anyone an explanation." His voice is gaining strength, and some color has returned to his cheeks. "I knew that eventually, someone would catch on. I just didn't imagine it would be a twelve year old girl!"

Before Sam has a chance to decide whether or not to be offended, Hunter and Cassy come running back into the boiler room, each holding a bottle of water left over from the pizza dinner upstairs.

"Here!" Cassy says, a bit winded. She approaches without hesitation and then smiles when Mr. Potts takes the water, thanking her politely.

Looking back over her shoulder, Sam notices how Hunter is choosing to linger at the far end of the room. She suspects that the years of ghost stories are battling with the real-life version in front of him, and he isn't fully convinced yet that the man isn't an apparition.

Mr. Potts guzzles the water, and it immediately helps to further improve his color. After clearing his throat, he wipes the remaining sweat from his forehead before looking intently at John.

"I understand if you still feel it necessary to notify the authorities," he states evenly. "I am, after all, trespassing."

John crosses his arms in response, and flashes a warm smile. "Sir, you've been coming here since you were a boy. There's a picture of your dad over there on the wall, and your wife still sits on the auxiliary for the school. I think it would be a stretch to say that you're doing anything wrong."

"You mean, aside from felony fraud?"

"What do you mean?" Cassy questions. "It's illegal to fake your own death?"

"No." Mr. Potts rises to his feet, still a little shaky. "It actually *isn't* illegal. However, a case could be made against us for the business dealings afterwards, including my life insurance payout." Shaking his head, he is obviously upset by the admission, but his previously slouched shoulders are now square as if a weight has been lifted. "I'd rather not discuss it any further if you don't mind," he continues. "Not without Grace present. If you aren't going to call the police, do you think I could trouble you for a ride back up to the house? I'm afraid I'm still a little too weak to make the hike."

Sam watches silently as John and Ally each take one of his arms, and they slowly work their way back towards the gym. As she passes Hunter, he steps in behind her and Cassy. While there are at least three different jokes about his irrational fear itching to come out, she holds back. Things are still a little too weird to be making light of it, and Sam hopes that Grace has some answers that make sense.

***

"Benjamin Thaddeus Potts, now we have *children* involved? How could we have let this go so far? We have no choice now but to turn ourselves in!"

Sam has a sneaking suspicion that Grace only calls her husband by his full name when she's upset. Because she is definitely upset.

The driveway that Mr. Potts directed them to take around the back of the house delivered them to the mudroom, and they're now gathered in the large kitchen. When Grace saw them, her face clouded and Sam was certain she would order them to leave. However, she's more defeated and apologetic than angry, though her frustration with the situation is clear.

"Now, Grace, you haven't given me a chance to even explain. I was in the boiler room. I had no intention of running into your friends. In fact, I think that they may have set me up."

Grace immediately looks at Sam, and she begins to squirm. "He's right, she admits. "I saw his things by the back door the first time we were here, and then couldn't help but notice the pairs of dishes in the sink."

"And the cologne," Cassy adds.

"Cologne?" Mr. Potts looks questioningly at Sam, an eyebrow raised.

"Umm, yeah. It's the same brand my dad wears. I noticed it here in the hall, and then down in the basement at the school. I don't believe in coincidences," she adds, when it doesn't sound like a good enough explanation.

To Sam's surprise, the older man begins to laugh. Slapping at his thigh, he looks at his wife and then spreads his arms wide. "After all this time, Grace, did you ever think my *cologne* would be what did us in?"

Sam flinches at this, and looks desperately between them. "But we won't tell anyone!" she promises, without thinking it through. "I'm sure you must have a really good reason for doing it."

"Sam." Walking over to her, Grace puts an

arm across her shoulders. "I appreciate your faith in us, and we actually *do* have a good reason, but it still wouldn't justify asking you kids to keep this kind of a secret. It would be very wrong, and I simply won't do it."

Sam's trying to think of a response when there's a loud knock at the front door. Visibly tensing, Grace looks fearfully at her husband, and Sam hates to think how she's imaging the police on the front step, there to arrest them. There has to be something they can do!

"It's just Sam's brother, Hunter," Cassy assures Grace. "He had to take the trail here, to make enough room in the car for Mr. Potts. I'll go let him in!"

While it's obvious that Mrs. Potts is relieved by the news, she's further distraught that yet another teen is being dragged into things.

"Before anything is decided," Sam rushes to say, holding the older woman's arm to keep her from moving toward the phone on the nearby counter. "Do you think you can at least tell us what happened? We aren't due home yet, and I would really like to know the whole story."

Hesitating slightly, Grace looks around at the

curious faces and then sighs in defeat. "Okay, I suppose we *do* owe you the truth. Let's go to the sitting room though, so Benny can warm up in front of the fire. He hasn't been well."

They follow the couple into the other room, and Hunter's mood improves when he discovers a plate of cookies on the coffee table. The girls take up their spot on the lounge, with John and Hunter opposite them. Sam thinks how nice it is to see Mr. Potts sitting next to wife, and wishes again that things were different.

"Mr. Potts, how have you stayed hidden all these years?" John takes a bite from a cookie, and then sits back in anticipation of his answer.

"Please, call me Ben. After six years, it's nice to hear my name." Taking a long breath, Ben closes his eyes for moment, trying to decide where to start. Looking up at the clock over the mantel, he then leans forward with his elbows on his knees.

"It's getting late, so I'll give you the condensed version. My business was my life. Our life," he adds, looking at Grace, who gives a tired smile in return. "We put all we had into it, but it wasn't enough. I made some poor investment choices and we found ourselves in trouble.

"We thought we were lucky to have a friend like Gregory Kingsman. He was a local man with strong business ties and knew how to turn things around financially. When I confided in him, he offered to take over the accounting from Grace, who was more than happy to give it up. That was our first mistake.

"The following year, after months of allowing him to manage the finances, he announced that the company was too far gone to rescue. At the time, I was developing my new wood product and was close to going for a patent to legally claim it as my own. When I showed it to him, he became very excited and encouraged me to submit it to a large corporation for backing. He convinced me that it would be a mistake not to go wide with it. With proper funding, he said it could be just what we needed to not only save the company, but much, much more.

"So I gave him the documents. The bulk of my work for nearly two years. It was less than a month later that he delivered the devastating news. Not only were they uninterested, but they claimed my research was flawed and that the product wasn't producible. I was devastated. That was our last chance. The company was going bankrupt and our friends that invested in our charities and other programs for decades were going to be financially ruined as well.

"By this time, Gregory had entered the political arena. He was campaigning hard for his first government seat. A month before we would be forced to file bankruptcy, I became suspicious of some of his dealings. It didn't take much digging to figure out that he'd been lying to me. He wasn't helping us at all, but stealing from us!

"At the time, I was too naïve to do the right thing. I still wanted to believe that he was my friend, so I confronted him about it and gave him a chance to confess and make things right. He pretended to be apologetic and was eager to make amends. He promised to return the money and fix everything. I gave him a week.

"What he proceeded to do was destroy all evidence of his ever being involved. He then came here to our house, spread out all the documents, and explained to us how our only chance to save the business, our home, our charities and the financial welfare of our friends, was for me to fake my death. I'm ashamed to admit it, but I was distraught. I saw myself as a failure at everything and I simply didn't know what else to do. I had no proof to go to anyone with. He was a highly respected man in the community. A rising star."

"We *did* try," Grace nearly whispers. Looking down at her hands, she wrings them nervously. "He's a dangerous man who'll stop at nothing to get what he wants. Ben stumbled upon some shady dealings that involved other politicians." Shuddering, Grace shifts closer to the fire. "When we at first refused to do what he asked, and threatened to expose him, he … well, he implied that Benny *would* disappear. It was up to us whether we were a part of the plan or not."

"I was a coward." Ben shakes his head and looks dejectedly at the group. "I was scared of what would happen to Grace. I didn't know what else to do."

"You were *forced* to do it!" Ally cries, feeling awful for the older couple. "He practically threatened to kill you if you didn't!"

"But I took the life insurance money, the bailout money from Kingsman, and played along with it," Grace confesses. "How is that going to look to the police? Without any proof, all of this will come back to us as insurance fraud. They'll never bring charges against that man."

"We found some recent articles about him," Cassy says, her brown eyes sparkling in the firelight. "You wouldn't be the first to claim that he's less than honest."

"And what about your invention?" Sam asks. "Did you know that he's been selling it as his own for years now?"

"Yes, I know." Hanging his head, the topic is clearly painful for Ben. "He stole that from me, too. He lied, and never really submitted it for me. A year after my disappearance, he claimed it as his own creation, patented it, and is now making millions. Gregory formed a separate business for the wood product, and now sells it through various channels. Of course, he destroyed any evidence that it was mine long ago. The only papers here at the house are my original hand drawings, and those don't prove anything."

"What about your boat?" Sam asks, her voice eager. "If you could show that wreck from six years ago, wouldn't that be enough to prove you made the product before Kingsman even trademarked it?"

Benjamin Potts stares thoughtfully at the young lady seated before him for a full minute before shaking his head ruefully. "Perhaps, Sam. It certainly wouldn't hurt our case, but I doubt it would be enough. No," he says with more surety. "The time to go to the authorities is long overdue."

"Plus, Benny needs medical care," Grace explains. Her husband scowls, but it doesn't silence her. "His health has been rapidly failing this past year. We suspect he has something wrong with his heart. I've been doing what I can to get our affairs in order. It's likely I'll be sentenced to some jail time, and I'm doing my best to protect the charities if that happens. I have the bank documents for the afterschool program, since that's still in my name, but Kingsman has forbid me from being directly involved. I can only see the money coming in and going out, so I have no way of knowing what he's really done with the funds. If I can figure that out, and get the other bank accounts signed over to the appropriate board members, we'll be more than ready to end this charade."

"How much time do you need to finish those things?" Ally asks.

"No more than a week," Grace answers. "But like I already said, having you involved in our secret is not acceptable."

"Grace, we've suspected it for several days. You've been doing this for six *years*. A few more days isn't going to make a difference." Sam hopes that she'll agree, but then realizes Mrs. Potts isn't the only one that needs convincing. Looking across the table, she meets John's stare and to her relief, he gives her a small, affirming nod. Hunter looks indifferent to it all, and is working on what's probably his fifth cookie.

"I don't know." It's clear that their host is wavering, looking at her husband, and then back at Sam.

The clock over the mantle chimes, reminding them all that it's eight o'clock at night. They need to leave soon. Sam already texted her mom that they were stopping by Mrs. Potts' house before coming home, but it's getting late.

"I guess it won't hurt to wait until after the haunted house, so that your benefit isn't ruined."

There's a collective sigh of relief, but Grace is quick to add more conditions. "If your parents ask you anything, you tell them the truth! I won't have anyone else lying for us. Do you understand?"

"Yes, ma'am," John assures her. "We wouldn't lie to them, anyways."

They all say goodbye before Grace can change her mind, and as they walk back through the kitchen, Ally quietly links arms with Sam. It's something they've done for years, and the motion calms her. Her jumbled up thoughts instantly fall into place, and she knows without a doubt that they *have* to find a way to prove that Gregory Kingsman is a fraud. And they have six days to do it.

11

EVIDENCE

"Hello, girls! Did your teacher give you my message? I didn't realize you were going to come by so soon."

Mrs. Trent, the afterschool program director, stands up from behind her desk as she's talking, and motions for them to come inside the spacious office.

"Yes, Miss. Covington told us you have some raffle tickets we can sell for admission to the haunted house," Sam replies, almost forgetting to use Lisa's formal name.

"Thank you, Kim," Mrs. Trent says, dismissing the teen still standing in the doorway, where she's lingered after escorting the girls to the office.

"I have a whole roll of tickets left over from a craft fair," she continues, refocusing on Sam. "Plus, when I was digging them out, I found a large inflatable spider and I instantly thought of you!"

"That would be perfect to hang at the entrance!" Cassy exclaims, clapping her hands together.

"Thanks, Mrs. Trent," Ally says sincerely. "And we can come back later if you're busy right now. We're just excited to start selling advance tickets!"

Sam notices the stacks of papers set out on the director's desk for the first time, surrounding a computer. There's also a calculator with a long expanse of printed numbers streaming from it. Mrs. Trent is obviously in the middle of some serious accounting work. Based on the number of crumpled up pieces of paper littering the floor, it isn't going very well.

"No, no, it's fine," she assures them, coming around and leaning back against the front of the messy desk. "I could use a break from all of this. I know that Kim shared our ... situation with you. It falls on my shoulders to try to come up with a way to make the numbers work, but -" Shaking her head, the director seems to realize what she was about to say and thinks better of it. "Never mind all of that! I didn't pull those items out of storage, but it won't take me long to get them. You girls can wait here. I shouldn't be longer than five or ten minutes."

As Mrs. Trent walks briskly from the office, Sam and Ally exchange a knowing look. Cassy is the first to voice their fears.

"That didn't sound good," the young girl says softly. Kicking at one of the wadded up papers, it tumbles across the floor and bounces against Sam's foot.

Reaching down, Sam picks it up without much thought, and smooths the paper out on her thigh. Bold letter across the top announce that It's a memo from the office of Mr. Gregory Kingsman. Her brows furrowing together, Sam studies the rest of the letter, and then in shock, reads it out loud for Ally and Cassy.

From: Gregory Kingsman
To: Director Susan Trent
Subject: Cease and Desist orders for the Ocean
            Side Afterschool Program

Dear Mrs. Trent:

It has come to my attention, that in spite of our detailed conversation this past Monday, on October 20th, you have continued to operate the Ocean Side Afterschool Program within its normal parameters.

Per our conversation, as well as the letter I presented to you, dated the same day, you are to immediately begin the process of terminating all extracurricular activities, and letting staff go. The end date of said program is the 28th of November, which gives you one month to reconcile all of the accounts, disburse the balances back to me, and send out notifications to the students.

I expect these orders to be followed post haste, or else I will be forced to replace you, per our discussion. I know it is important to you to see the closure through yourself, so I will expect your immediate compliance.

With best of wishes,

Gregory Kingsman

Sam continues to stare at the thick, expensive stationary. Looking again at the dates, she realizes that with the Potts' revelation this coming weekend, the program won't stand a chance. It's already Thursday. While they've managed to finish the rest of the work on the haunted house, they haven't heard anything from Mr. and Mrs. Potts.

It's been easy to avoid having to tell their parents or Lisa about Benjamin, because it simply isn't a topic that they would bring up on their own. He's been considered dead for six years. Sam is still tempted to confess it all to her mom anyways, and she knows that her friends have similar thoughts. She figures her parents might be able to come up with a way of helping them, but the likelihood is that they'd just report it to the authorities instead.

Sighing with frustration, Sam wishes there were something more they could do. At the sound of more paper rustling, she looks up to find Cassy studying another one of the discarded documents.

"It looks like this must be the first letter he sent," she says, handing it to Sam.

"This one is just a bunch of numbers," Ally adds, holding another piece of paper. "But I don't think we should be doing this," she adds nervously, handing it off quickly to Sam.

Ally has a valid point, but an idea has begun to wiggle its way into Sam's thoughts and she can't shake it off. "Grace said that she has the bank statements for the funding for the program, but can't prove what Kingsman is doing with the money, because she doesn't have access to this," she states, shaking the paper with all the numbers on it.

"It looks like Mrs. Trent is trying to figure out the balances of the various accounts, like Kingsman asked her to do," Sam continues, standing now and moving over to the desk. "These might be exactly what Grace needs, to prove that Mr. Kingsman is stealing the money!"

"Give me your phone," Cassy suddenly demands, coming to stand next to Sam.

Sam complies without question, pulling her smartphone from her back pocket. While Cassy has a cellphone, it's a much older style without a touchscreen. She only went to live with Lisa Covington less than two months ago, and hasn't upgraded yet.

Watching with growing astonishment, Ally realizes that Cassy is going to take *pictures* of the documents! "What are you doing?" she gasps, looking back fretfully at the open door. "Mrs. Trent could be back any minute!"

Crumpling the papers back up after Cassy snaps the picture; Sam tosses them onto the floor before looking at Ally. "This is the Potts' program, *not* Kingsman's!" she says urgently, pulling another promising looking paper from the top of a pile and handing it to Cassy. "Grace would come in here and do this herself, if it weren't for that crook blackmailing her! We aren't doing anything wrong," she emphasizes, as much for own conscience as for Ally's benefit.

Cassy takes three more pictures of what look to be the most important papers, and then also one of the file currently open on the monitor, before rushing back around the desk. Grabbing Sam's arm as she goes, she drags her back to the empty chairs, and they sit down just as Mrs. Trent enters the room.

Sam was so absorbed, that she wasn't listening for the telltale footsteps. Looking at

Cassy thankfully, she hopes that Ally isn't too mad. Glancing briefly at her best friend as Mrs. Trent approaches them, she's relieved to see her turn and greet the director as if nothing has happened.

"Here you go!" Mrs. Trent says cheerfully. She's put the big roll of tickets and inflatable insect in a paper bag, which Ally takes from her with a smile.

"This is going to be great!" Cassy says, rising from her seat. "We hope that you'll come."

"How many kids are in the program?" Sam asks, walking over to Ally and pulling the tickets out of the bag.

"Forty right now," Mrs. Trent answers, her demeanor changing slightly at the reminder that soon, there won't be any.

"Here." Sam tears off a handful of tickets, and gives them to the older woman. "We planned on making special invitations, but didn't have time. Can you hand these out to them this week? We would love to have all of the kids come!"

Smiling again, Mrs. Trent accepts the coupons, and then walks the girls out to the front entrance. "We'll look forward to seeing you on

Saturday," she tells them sincerely. "I'm sure it will be amazing!"

Once outside, Sam squints against the bright, afternoon sunshine. As her eyes adjust, she nearly bumps into someone coming up the steps.

"Excuse me, young lady!"

Looking up at the deep voice, Sam instantly recognizes Gregory Kingsman. Although he's wearing jeans and a t-shirt instead of a suit, his slicked back hair and fake smile are hard to miss.

He's holding a large, manila envelope in his hand, and Sam wonders if it's another threatening memo for poor Mrs. Trent. The thought angers her, and she answers with a bit more vehemence than intended. "Well, excuse *me*."

Stepping around him, she rushes to catch up with Ally and Cassy at the bottom of the broad steps, the back of her neck burning from her flush of annoyance.

"Wait. Do I know you? Perhaps I can help you with something?"

Turning back, Sam tries to gather herself. They're so close to possibly putting an end to his manipulation that she doesn't want to ruin things now. "I don't think we've ever met, sir. We belong to a charity club at the middle school, and we're hosting a fundraiser for the afterschool program this weekend."

His face goes through a transformation, from the proper politician, to a darker, more sinister adversary. "Ahhh, yes. The haunted house." He says it with disdain, while slowly descending two of the steps, moving closer. "Mrs. Trent told me all about it. You must be the infamous Samantha Wolf."

Sam can't help but take a step back. It's unsettling that he knows her name.

"I remember reading an article this summer, regarding one of your escapades. You seem to have a knack for getting yourself into trouble. You know, I'm close friends with Grace Potts. I hope your event is a big success. But so many things can go wrong with these types of … undertakings."

Biting back a response, Sam doesn't dare look away first. It isn't until Ally grabs her by the shoulders that she finally turns around. The three girls walk away silently, leaving the slimy man grinning on the porch.

Resisting the urge to run, Sam instead pats

the phone now secured in her back pocket. On it is what she hopes is the information needed to keep the Potts out of jail, and to take Gregory Kingsman down.

12

ROADBLOCK

The hike up the hill seems to be taking a whole lot longer than usual. Sam is nervous, and she knows that Ally and Cassy are, too. Grace gave them strict orders not to do anything to try to help them, and they're about to give her proof of doing just that.

They went back to Ally's last night, after the confrontation with Kingsman, and printed out the pictures from Sam's phone. Now, the evidence is folded in her back pocket, where it's been all day at school. Their excuse for the visit this Friday afternoon is to give Grace some tickets, and to show her the final plans for the haunted house. All valid reasons.

"Do you think Grace and Benjamin will be mad?" Ally whispers her question, as if fearful that someone might overhear her on the wooded trail.

"I hope not," Sam answers. Looking up at the bright blue, fall sky, she takes in a deep breath of the crisp air and tries to calm her nerves.

The girls already had this discussion the night before, and decided that it was worth taking the chance. At least this way they know they've done everything possible to help.

"We really do need to hurry," Cassy urges from farther up the path. "Lisa will be done grading her papers by four. If we're going to get home in time for dinner before the football game, we have to get back to the school and catch a ride with her."

The boys have a home game tonight, and the girls promised that they would be there for it. Hunter even thinks he might have a chance of getting in on the punt return team, a sort of rites of passage for a junior varsity player.

It's almost three o'clock by the time they arrive, and Grace ushers them in. She greets them wearing an apron, with tantalizing smells escaping through the open door. She's in the middle of making a pot roast dinner, and directs the three girls to different spots along the counter in the spacious kitchen to help cut up vegetables.

Cassy gives the tickets to Grace first, and then they begin making small talk about the final layout for the haunted house while working. Sam tries to come up with a way to tell her about the evidence, as she's slicing up a carrot.

"Sam," Grace suddenly says, interrupting her thoughts. "Why don't you tell me why you're really here?"

Blushing, the young sleuth slowly wipes her damp hands on her jeans. Was she really that obvious? "Can we talk to Mr. Potts, too?" Sam asks, turning to face Grace. "We have something to show both of you."

Her smile fading, Grace pulls a chair out from the table and sits down. "I'm afraid not. Benny hasn't been doing well at all the past couple of days. He's lying down right now, girls, and I'd rather not bother him."

The news gives weight to the need for action, and it encourages Sam that they're doing the right thing. Stepping away from the carrots with purpose, she goes to stand next to Grace, while pulling the sheets of paper from her back pocket.

Ally and Cassy exchange a nervous look. Ally isn't so confident, but she has faith in Sam. Her friend has a knack for putting random pieces of information together where others don't see the pattern. She's also much braver than your average teen, and doesn't hesitate to push, where others might back away. If anyone can convince Grace to let the girls help, it's her.

Spreading the pages out deliberately on the kitchen table, Sam then sits down in the other chair. She nervously picks at the ragged edges of a new hole in her jeans, while Grace looks over the documents.

"What is this?"

Sam looks up at the sharp intake of breath, and cringes at the disapproving frown on Grace's face. "We stopped by the program yesterday to pick up some items from Mrs. Trent," she explains. "She was working on some stuff in her office, and it was pretty obvious that she was upset about it. When she left to go get the things for us, we happened to look at one of the papers she crumpled up and threw on the floor. We weren't trying to be nosey," Sam adds hastily, as the older woman begins to shake her head in displeasure. "But I thought that these numbers might be what you need to compare to your bank statements, and prove that Mr. Kingsman is taking the money!"

Grace starts to say something, but then thinks better of it, and presses her lips together in a hard line. Standing abruptly, she gathers the papers up and walks briskly from the room without a word.

The three girls are left staring at each other in uncertainty. Cassy and Ally are frozen at first, but then go and stand on either side of Sam. An old clock mounted on the wall above the table ticks off the seconds, suddenly much louder than before, in the now silent room.

"Should we leave?" Ally finally whispers, when several minutes pass without any sign of Mrs. Potts.

Shaking her head, Sam stands and pushes her chair in. The legs scrape across the floor and seem to break the spell. "No. I don't want to leave without talking to her some more. We just *have* to figure out a way to prove their innocence!"

Approaching footsteps announce Grace's return, and she walks back into the kitchen with a cardboard box in her arms. Setting it on the table, she then looks pointedly at Sam.

"These are all of the bank statements for the past year," she explains, taking out a handful of official looking papers. "I have to admit that I haven't really done much with them, other than to put them in this box. I've felt completely helpless, and haven't seen the point in doing much else.

"But things are different now," she continues, making separate stacks and beginning to sort the documents while talking. "Even if you hadn't found Benny, we don't have a choice. I won't risk his health any longer. The truth has to come out. At least now, we have a chance to prove what Gregory has been doing. He's known all along that if Benny survived that storm, he'd have to cover his involvement … and he has. I have no doubt now that that thief intended for my Benny to drown. He *knew* that storm was going to hit early, and it's why he pushed him to go that day."

Pounding a fist on the table, Grace looks up at Sam, her face a combination of anger and grief. "He's threatened, blackmailed, and stolen from us consistently for the past six years, but I'm afraid we're not going to have enough to prove it!"

Sitting down again, Sam takes her older friends' hand in her own, and squeezes it reassuringly. "Maybe his crooked dealings with the afterschool program will be enough to make the authorities look more closely at all of his other transactions," she says, trying to sound reassuring.

"Perhaps," Grace replies, forcing a smile. "Whatever the outcome, I must insist that you girls not involve yourself any further."

Sam tries to respond, but Mrs. Potts drops her hand and surprises her by firmly grasping her arms. "I mean it, Sam. No more. I appreciate your caring enough to want to help us, but this has gone way too far. I will *not* have you mixed up in *any* of this! Do you understand? You host the fundraiser tomorrow night, Sunday I will phone the police, and that will be the end of it."

On the verge of tears, Sam looks numbly at

Grace, unsure of how to respond. Even though she wants to do more to help, she can't think of a way to do it, so it'll be easy to follow her demand.

"We understand, Grace," Ally offers, wiping at her nose. Always the more emotional one, she's unable to hold her own tears back.

"Sam?" Grace asks, still unconvinced.

"Of course," Sam finally mumbles. Grace releases her arms, but then leans in to give her young friend a brief but fierce hug.

13

GOOD DEEDS GONE WRONG

Sam tugs at the eye patch and pulls the elastic up, turning it into a makeshift hairband. "I guess my head must be bigger than Hunter's," she complains, rubbing at the mark it's made on her left temple. Borrowing her brother's pirate costume from last year seemed like a good idea, but now she's not so sure.

"I know I'm missing a perfect opportunity right now to make a joke about brain size," Cassy counters, looking at her own ghostly white face in the school bathroom mirror, "but I'm too exhausted to think that hard." Deciding it's not quite Casper-like yet, she dabs some more face paint on, and then stands back to admire her reflection. "What do you think?"

Sam tugs at her oversized, black and white striped pirate shirt, before studying Cassy's handiwork. "If you're going for a friendly ghost, you might want to rethink the black eyeliner and bloody lips," she offers, reaching out to wipe off a clump of paint from Cassy's ear.

Laughing, Cassy twirls around, making her white flowing robes balloon out, and does her best imitation of a scary moan. "I dunno. At first, I thought that since I'm going to be taking and selling the tickets, I should look friendly, but I'm kinda liking the whole spook thing."

"Go for it!" Ally urges, already gathering the makeup back into a bag. "Your dark hair looks fabulous against the white. "You look like one of those freaky things crawling out from under a bed in a horror movie."

"Ummm … I dunno if that's a compliment or not," Cassy counters. "You, on the other hand, are absolutely terrifying. If anyone goes running out of there, we'll know why!"

Ally pats at her red hair, which is teased and sprayed so that it sticks nearly straight out from her head. Her clown makeup is perfect, and all she needs to do is put on the big red nose to complete her outfit. While Sam is escorting the paying guests through the maze of scares, Ally will be stationed about midway through, in a dark corner. Propped up like an oversized doll, as people stroll by she'll come to life and chase after them.

"It's not even two-thirty yet, but it feels like midnight!" Sam complains, following Ally out of the locker room. "But at least we have some time to relax."

John and Hunter got permission from their coach to use their football gear as part of their zombie costumes, but in exchange, they have to participate in the whole Saturday practice. It doesn't get over until three-thirty, but one of their teammates claims to be a pro at zombie makeup and is going to do theirs before they leave the high school.

As a result, the set-up time was moved to eight that morning, so most of the work was done when the guys left at noon. With the help of the other students that showed up at eleven, everything that could be finished in advance is completed. Lisa is leaving at four to go pick up a bunch of dry ice, and one of the boys in the club, Brian, is bringing his two promised smoke machines.

Sam stands back to observe the entrance, trying to picture it with the smoke, dry ice fog and black lights. She has to admit that it's all come together a lot better than she ever hoped, but it's hard to be too happy with the nagging thoughts of Grace and Benjamin Potts tugging at her.

"Something is still missing," Ally observes, tapping at her chin.

Sam didn't even realize that her friends were standing beside her, and jumps at the comment. Laughing at herself, she tries to shake off her mood, and to focus instead on the upcoming, positive night. "What else could we possibly cram in there? I don't think we can get one more decoration in it."

"No, we have *plenty* of decorations," Ally agrees. "I'm talking about the reason *why* we're doing it. We've got all the signs up that we made to advertise the haunted house, but nothing about the afterschool program. We need a donation table, and information board!" she says, getting more excited. "So that people know what their money is going to. I helped with a fundraiser once at our church. It was a kid's camp, and they put this big board up with all sorts of pictures of the camp and the name. Then, there was a jar where people could give extra money."

"That's a wonderful idea, Ally!" Lisa agrees, walking over with empty bags of fake cobwebs. "We could pull out one of the folding tables, and put it over by the entrance, across from the ticket table."

"But what would we put on the board?" Cassy questions. "We don't really have anything."

"We've got all sorts of craft paper and paint," Sam says, thinking aloud. "It would be easy enough to use some of the left over cardboard, decorate it, and paint the name across the top."

"We have over two hours until we really need to be back here," Ally continues. "We can go take some pictures of the school and get them developed at the hour developing place just down the street. We'd have plenty of time to set it up!"

"Here," Lisa offers, pulling out her wallet.

"This should be enough to pay for several photos, and some sandwiches while you wait. I'll work on getting the rest of this picked up, and then I'll go write up some information about the program and print it out on the computer in my classroom."

After a brief debate about walking around town in their costumes, the girls decide that it *is* Halloween, after all.

It doesn't take long to make their way to the building, and Sam snaps off some quick pictures of the quaint porch and sign.

"Why don't we walk around back and get some shots of the cute playground?" Ally suggests. "I just wish we thought of it when we were here with the kids."

As they push through the latched side gate, Sam moves forward to get a good view of the outdoor toys, while Cassy asks to borrow Ally's phone. "I'm pretty sure they have a website," she explains, doing a search on the internet. "Here! I found it. There are all sorts of pictures on here. I'm sure we can download and use some of them."

"Aren't they protected by a trademark, or

something?" Sam asks, unsure of using the photos without permission.

"You mean a copyright," Ally corrects, taking her phone back. "My Dad explained all of that to me once. Since we're doing this fundraiser with the permission of the school, I'm sure it'll be okay to use their pictures. We'll just have to give them credit for it on the board somewhere. And we really shouldn't use one if you can see the kids' faces. A trademark," she continues, slipping on to one of the swings, "is what you see stamped on a product, like a hairbrush or something."

Joining Ally, Sam, and Cassy both sit on the other two empty swings. Twirling slowly, Sam suddenly sits up straight, a faraway look on her face. "A trademark …"

"Uh-oh," Cassy murmurs, beginning to recognize the same warning signs that Ally has spoken of several times. Their friend is onto something.

Jumping down from the swing, Sam starts thumbing frantically through her pictures. "Where is it … here!" Still talking to herself, she takes a few steps forward so she can see the image better in the shade of the building. Swiping at the screen, she enlarges the picture and then gasps. "Look!"

Her excitement rubbing off on them, Ally and Cassy scramble to Sam's side, and lean in close to her phone. It's the picture that she took at the pirate cove. The close-up shot of the fabricated wood used to make Benjamin Potts' ill-fated boat. Sam has enlarged it to the point that the screen is dark with it, but in the middle, barely visible, is what looks to be a raised edge clearly forming the letters B T P.

"That has to be Benjamin Thaddeus Potts Trademark!" Ally cries, looking up at Sam in amazement. "He might not have submitted his work for a legal patent, but he still stamped it to identify it as his."

"You mean we can prove that the fake wood in the pirate's cove is from his boat?" Cassy asks, trying to grasp the bigger picture.

Nodding, Sam swallows around the lump rising in her throat. "Not only that, Cassy, but we can prove that Mr. Potts invented that wood over a year before Gregory Kingsman stole it! *This* is what they need to prove *everything*!"

"We'll have John take us out there tomorrow morning," Ally says, tapping out a rapid-fire text message to her brother while she's talking. "We might even be able to get it back in time for the Potts to show to the police! They'll be so surprised!"

"Why wait until tomorrow?"

Spinning around at the deep voice coming from the shadows of the porch behind them, the three girls all cry out in fear. Standing there is Gregory Kingsman!

"It's a beautiful day for a treasure hunt," he says coyly, and begins to walk slowly towards them.

14

AYE, MATIES!

Ally grabs onto Sam's hand instinctively, pulling her friend close. Cassy crowds her other side, and together, the three of them face the large, intimidating man.

"We should be going," Sam says bravely. "We're expected back at the school." Her voice wavers slightly, and she hopes that her lie isn't too transparent.

Mr. Kingsman is standing in between them and the only exit from the backyard area. The building wraps around three sides of them, creating the courtyard, with the fence and bushes closing it off from the side street. Even if the door he came out didn't lock behind him, they would still have to go around the man to get to it.

He must have been in the office, and heard us talking out here, Sam thinks, chastising herself for not paying more attention to any cars parked out on the road. They should have knocked on the front door first, before coming back here. *How much did he hear?*

Sticking out his hand, any trace of humor fades from his face as his eyes narrow to slits. "Give me your phones."

Sam takes an automatic step back from him, bumping into Ally. Her phone still grasped in her now clammy hand, she can't try to claim not to have one. Hesitating, she looks sideways at Ally, unsure of what to do. *Why does he want their phones?*

Ally stares back at Sam, just as confused by the request as she is. Clearing her throat, Ally leans in close to her. "Let's just leave," she whispers, somewhat desperate. "What's he going to do, tackle all of us?"

Cassy surprises both girls by stepping past them, her white robe flapping in the offshore breeze. When Kingsman doesn't move aside for her, she stops just a couple of feet short, crossing her arms over her chest. "We aren't doing anything wrong."

"You're trespassing," he replies with authority. "Now give me your phones!"

Cassy flinches as he yells at her, but doesn't back down. "We have permission to be here, and my sister isn't going to like the way you're talking to us!" Instead of following his demand, she flips open her older cellphone and starts to dial Lisa's number.

In a motion so fast that Sam barely has time to react, Kingsman steps forward and slaps the phone from Cassy's hand, sending it crashing against the side of the building. Cassy gasps and falls away from him, as pieces of her phone clatter to the deck.

Reaching out to catch the shocked girl, Sam and Cassy then stumble back, a contrast of black and white material tumbling to the ground. Sam's phone bounces across the yard, knocked free by the impact.

Left standing alone, Ally trembles slightly when Kingsman advances on her. Holding her hand out, she offers the cell to him, and then recoils as he snatches it away.

Watching the scene with dismay, Sam notes

that in a different setting, the stunned expression on her friend's clown-painted face might be funny. However, it's rapidly becoming apparent that Gregory Kingsman heard *everything* they said, and he has a lot to lose. How far is the rising politician willing to go to keep his secrets?

"What's going on, boss?"

Rising slowly to her feet, tying to think of a way out of the situation, Sam spots the man that's appeared at the gate. He's younger than Kingsman, probably in his late twenties. He's dressed more casually in a worn t-shirt and his hair is overgrown and unkempt.

"Here," Gregory barks, tossing Ally's phone at him. Bending to pick up Sam's, he throws that at him, too. "Lock these in the glovebox, Ryan, and then bring the car around. We've got a change in plans."

Ryan looks at the older man questioningly, but he doesn't appear troubled by the requests. "Sure, man. Whatever you want. But what's with the kids?"

"They stuck their noses where they shouldn't have," Kingsman explains evenly.

Shrugging, the younger man doesn't push for

more information, and Sam is discouraged when he leaves, apparently to go get the car. It doesn't seem that he's going to help them.

Sam pulls Cassy to her feet, and she notices fresh grass stains on her white costume. The evidence of the attack against her friend causes a wave of anger to wash over Sam, and propels her into action. If they're going to get away, it has to happen before Ryan returns.

Rushing forward, Sam dodges around the surprised man when he reaches for her, leaping for the gate. Her hand finds purchase with the latch and she's beginning to think she might get away, when a vice-like grip pulls her arm back. Crying out in frustration more than pain, Sam starts to yell for help, but is cut off abruptly by a large hand clamped over her mouth!

Spinning her around at the same time, Gregory now has her right arm twisted up behind her, forcing her to face her terrified friends.

"You are all going to do *exactly* what I tell you!"

Shoving Sam forward for emphasis, she cries out in response, her scream muffled behind his fingers.

"No one has to get hurt," he continues, perhaps realizing he might be taking things too far. "You're going to take me to the wreckage. I'm going to get what I need, and then you all can go back and play haunted house like nothing ever happened. Understand?"

Ally and Cassy look at each other, desperate to agree with whatever it takes to make him let go of Sam.

"Sure," Ally croaks, her voice breaking under the stress. "We'll show you where it is, just leave her alone!"

The sound of crunching gravel announces Ryan's return with the car. Kicking the gate open, Gregory looks behind him to make sure the way is clear.

"Not a sound, understand?" he says menacingly, close to Sam's face.

Nodding deliberately, Sam then hungrily gulps in fresh air when he removes his hand. Propelled forward by the powerful grip on her arm, she stumbles up to the open passenger door of the slick, black car. Sam can see other vehicles passing by, down on the main road, but the alley is empty. There's no one to help them.

****

The irony of her choice of costume as they enter the trail to the pirate cove isn't lost on Sam. Tugging again at her eye patch, she looks back at the parking lot, empty except for their car. It isn't a well-known trail system, and this late in the season, it's not surprising that they're the only ones here.

Gregory is leading the way, eager to reach their final destination. Cassy, Ally, and Sam are clustered close together, with Ryan lagging behind. He appears distracted by the woods. Although it's not even four yet, the sun is low on the horizon and shadows are already beginning to gather in the forest.

Looking down at the black eyepatch now clutched in her hand, and then back at Ryan, Sam nonchalantly tosses it to the side of the path as they pass the trailhead sign. Holding her breath until Ryan steps over it without noticing, she then closes her eyes and sends a silent prayer. Lisa will be wondering where they are by now, and she can imagine all the missed calls that have been going straight to voicemail. They'll be out looking for them soon, but she needs to slow things down.

Ten minutes later, they come up to the large rock that marks where they should veer off. As Cassy starts to call out, Sam quickly takes her hand and squeezes, silencing her. Ally doesn't need any encouraging and goes along with the deceit. After another fifteen minutes, Sam pretends to notice for the first time that they've gone too far.

Backtracking, Gregory eyes the girls suspiciously. "Make sure you don't have any more 'mistakes' or else your phones will end up in pieces, like the ghosts."

Cassy looks back at him sharply, her white face paint now drying and beginning to crack, causing her skin to itch. The phone might have been old, but it's one of the few things she still had from her grandmother, so the loss is personal.

The forest floor is spongy, covered in thick moss and large ferns that are growing at the base of fir and cedar trees. Even less light is filtered through here, creating an eerie landscape of deep greens speckled with iridescent rays of sunlight.

"I hope you at least brought a flashlight," Ryan says, breaking the cathedral-like silence. "'Cause you know it's going to be dark soon, right?" Looking panicked the younger man bats at a cedar branch hanging close to his head.

"Shut up," Kingsman orders, clearly not in the mood to deal with his whining. "How much farther?" he continues, looking at Sam suspiciously.

Deciding that she better not push her luck, Sam looks dejectedly at Ally before answering. "It's right up here," she mutters, stepping over a small log.

A few minutes later, the group of five emerges into the clearing, but the scene is so much different than before, that Sam is momentarily confused. The cove is covered in a thin layer of murky water, with the remnants of the boat barely visible on the far side.

"The tide must be extra high!" Cassy gasps, jumping back.

"Go!" Gregory shouts, not caring if they get wet and muddy.

The water is less than six inches deep through most of the cove, but is nearly a foot by the time they reach the 'pirate ship'. Cassy is holding her robe up, so that only her feet are wet, but the rest of them are submerged up to their knees.

"*This* is what all the fuss is about?" Ryan asks. Looking at the boards, he's clearly unimpressed.

"This 'fuss' could cost me millions," the older man explains, dropping a garbage bag from his shoulder that he took from the trunk of his car. From it, he pulls out a small crowbar and long handled screwdriver, items he rummaged from the vehicles' emergency kit that he thought might be useful. "That translates into a whole lot of money for you, too, kid ... so stop complaining and get to work!"

The three girls stand back, watching as the two men pry the old, flexible boards away from what's left of that section of the hull. Once he has a length removed, Gregory steps on one end of the four foot long plank and then pulls up on the other until it snaps in two with a loud *pop*. Dropping the two pieces into the bag, he then works on loosening the next one.

This continues for what has to be a half hour, and Sam, shivering from the combination of cold ocean water around her legs and the lowering sun, begins scanning the tree line. It's got to be almost five by now. What if no one figures out where they are? She doesn't trust that Mr. Kingsman is really going to just let them go back unscathed.

"There!" Ryan shouts, another *pop* echoing through the trees. "That's the last one. Can we get out of here now? I don't want to be here in the dark, man."

The clash of rapidly changing temperatures between the air, water, and humidity is causing a thin layer of ground fog to form. Sinuous tendrils of mist reach up from it, wrapping around their legs. In the fading light, Sam's anxiety grows to new levels, and the creep factor of her friends' Halloween costumes is *not* helping.

A flash of movement catches Sam's attention. On the other side of the cove, someone, or *something* is moving in between the trees. On the verge of screaming in fear, she starts to reach for Ally and Cassy, but then recognizes the reflective number seven. *John.*

The two older men are gathering their things and preparing to turn back in that direction. Frantic to distract them, Sam sloshes through the water, the fog exploding around her as she moves.

"What now?" she demands, trying to force much more strength into her voice than she actually feels. "You aren't really going to take us back to the haunted house. Are you." It isn't a question, and Sam's stomach clenches painfully.

When Kingsman only stares at her smugly, Ryan looks back and forth between them fretfully.

"Hey, man, I know this is important, but I ain't into hurting little girls."

"Relax, Ryan," the smooth talker croons. "I already told you that no one has to get hurt. But you're right, Sam," he continues, turning back to her and hefting the wet bag full of planks onto his shoulder. "We aren't going back to the school. You see, Ryan and I stopped by my office at the afterschool program this evening, and encountered some juvenile delinquents that broke into the place. Turns out you three have gotten quite close to that old quack, Mrs. Potts, and she's filled your head with a bunch of lies.

"They're a couple of con artists, you know, Grace and Benjamin." Chuckling now at his own cunning, Gregory Kingsman leans down slightly so that his face is level with Sam's. "Not only did they fake his death to get out from under losing everything and collecting on his life insurance, but they're low enough to brainwash some kids to do their bidding. Yup ... convinced you three to sneak into my office and set fire to the building, in order to destroy the evidence that they've been *continuing* to steal money from their own charity! Of course, Samantha is already known for getting into trouble, but maybe the judge will go easy on you, given your age."

"You can't!" Ally gasps, her pale hand flying to cover her red-painted mouth.

"You won't get away with it!" Cassy counters, leaning forward and dropping her robe into the water. "We won't let you!"

"Oh, but I think I will," Gregory says with more malice. Throwing the bag at Ryan, he then turns back to Sam in one smooth motion and takes ahold of both of her wrists. "Unless you all want to have an unfortunate *accident* here."

The mist has taken on an otherworldly glow in the twilight, so that when John suddenly explodes out of the woods to their right, his face painted up like a zombie, Gregory looks at him in horror before John slams into him. The collision is brutal, throwing all three of them into the water.

Hunter is close behind, and although smaller than John, the effect on the already spooked younger man is extreme. Screaming, Ryan turns and tries unsuccessfully to run through the knee-deep water. After only three steps, he plunges forward, disappearing briefly under the fog before coming up sputtering.

Ally and Cassy rush to pull Sam up from the frigid seawater, where she fell after being thrown free by the tackle. While John's football gear protected him from the brunt of the assault, Gregory isn't so fortunate. John stands over the older man, his face an odd mixture of undead makeup and anger, his shoulders heaving from his ragged breaths. Sam realizes that the boys must have run all the way there.

Still in the water, Kingsman is writhing in pain, holding his bruised ribs and trying to catch his breath. Just as he tries to push himself to his feet, the cove erupts with shouts and light as several police officers run towards them, flashlights dancing across the chaotic scene.

"You're finished," John shouts at his adversary, before stepping back.

Sam, holding tight to Ally and Cassy, realizes with relief that he's right. It's over. Looking at the garbage bag, its top barely visible above the mist, she smiles for the first time that night.

15

A HALLOWEEN TO REMEMBER

"When none of you were answering your phones, I called Lisa, and she said that you were going to the school program to take pictures," John explains.

The kids are all gathered in the front office of the middle school along with their parents, Lisa, and two police officers. Gregory and Ryan are on their way to the police station.

"When we found Cassy's broken phone," Hunter adds, continuing the story. "We figured something had to be wrong."

"I got ahold of your parents and we all began looking," Lisa says, hugging Cassy close.

"If it weren't for the text message Ally sent me, about having to go to the pirate cove," John urges, "Hunter and I would have never guessed to check there. When I saw your eye patch, Sam, I knew you must have dropped it on purpose, so we called the police."

"So does anyone want to explain why one of Ocean Sides' most successful businessmen, and up-and-coming politicians would force three young girls into the woods against their will?"

Nathan Wolf turns towards a new arrival, the town sheriff, now standing in the doorway. "That's a really good question," he replies, looking back at Sam. "I'd also like to know how my daughter managed to get into trouble *this* time."

Trying to shrink back into the hard plastic chair, Sam pulls the blanket that one of the officers gave her a little tighter under her chin. Glancing at her mom, she realizes with dread that this is going to be a tough one to explain.

"Don't blame Sam."

Sam jumps up from the chair at the unexpected arrival of Grace Potts, the blanket falling to the ground. Beside her, Ally gasps at the sight of Benjamin standing behind her!

The sheriff, very familiar with Grace Potts, turns to warmly greet the older woman, but takes a staggering step back when he sees Benjamin. "Ben!" he hollers, the color draining from his face, thinking he's looking at a ghost.

"It's okay, Sheriff Tucker," Ben says calmly, holding his hands up weakly. "Go ahead and sit down, though. I'm afraid that this is all somewhat convoluted."

During the moment of stunned silence, the sounds of laughter and people milling about can be heard floating down the hallway from the gym. With everyone safe and accounted for, the rest of the kids decided to go ahead with the fundraiser and it's drawing quite a crowd. Sam can't help but think how the people in *this* room are actually getting the bigger show.

It takes nearly an hour for the Potts to explain their story in detail, stopping periodically to emphasize how Sam and her friends only meant to help. When Grace concludes her side with the revelation of the bank statements from the day before, she turns the storytelling over to the preteens.

"We went to the afterschool program to take pictures, just like we said we would," Cassy confirms. "But after we went into the playground area, we were there talking about the pirate cove, and that's when Mr. Kingsman - "

"The what?" Sheriff Tucker interrupts.

"That's what the kids call the spot in the woods where the boat is," Ally's Dad answers, familiar with the location that his son had played at years before. He and Elizabeth Parker have been very quiet so far, having arrived at the school just before the sheriff.

"Gregory Kingsman heard us talking about how the ruins can prove that he's a liar!" Sam exclaims, searching out Benjamin Potts with the revelation. He meets her gaze, and she can see him puzzling over it, trying to figure out what she means. "Your *trademark*," she insists, while getting up to go to the bag that she begged the police to bring inside with them.

Sam tugs at the strings, causing the thick black plastic to fall away, revealing what looks to be a jumbled mess of weird planks. Looking through them, she selects one and then carries it over to the older man. Holding it out to him, he takes it from her without a word.

Slowly and methodically, Benjamin Potts examines the remains of his life's work, running his fingers over it until they slide across the raised mark at one end. Looking up at Sam, he begins to nod. Sighing, he slumps in the chair as if he were a hiker that finally reached the end of a very long journey.

Placing her hands ever so slowly over her heart, Grace's eyes well with tears as she smiles. "This is the proof we need," she says to the sheriff. "With it, we should be able to take back our company, and put Gregory Kingsman where he belongs. Thank you Sam," she continues, reaching out to squeeze her hand. "All of you. It means so much."

"It's going to take some time to work out the legalities of all of this," Sheriff Tucker counters, taking the 'evidence' from Mr. Potts. "But what I know right now, is that I have enough to hold Kingsman for kidnapping, and not a darn reason to take either one of you kind folks to jail. Instead, why don't I give you a lift to the hospital, Ben? I think you might be in need of some medical care."

Mr. Potts is happy to oblige, but not before hugging each of the girls first. As Sam leans in, she catches a whiff of a familiar scent, one that will forever remind her of the ghost of Eagle Creek Middle School.

THE END

Thank you for reading, 'The Haunting of Eagle Creek Middle School'! I hope that you enjoyed it, and will take the time to write a simple review on Amazon!

http://www.amazon.com/dp/B01FMTAKK8

Want to be notified when Tara releases a new novel? Sign up now for her newsletter! eepurl.com/bzdHA5

*Be sure to look for Sam and Ally in other exciting adventures in **The Samantha Wolf Mysteries**!*

ABOUT THE AUTHOR

Author Tara Ellis lives in a small town in beautiful Washington State, in the Pacific Northwest. She enjoys the quiet lifestyle with her two teenage kids, and several dogs. Tara was a firefighter/EMT, and worked in the medical field for many years. She now teaches CPR, and concentrates on family, photography, and writing middle grade and young adult novels.

Visit her author page on Amazon to find all of her books!

http://www.amazon.com/author/taraellis